Tree.

Table.

Book.

Tree.

Table.

Book.

LOIS LOWRY

Clarion Books
An Imprint of HarperCollinsPublishers

Library of Congress Cataloging-in-Publication Data
Names: Lowry, Lois, author.
Title: Tree. Table. Book. / Lois Lowry.
Description: First edition. | New York : Clarion Books, [2024] | Audience:
Ages 8–12. | Audience: Grades 4–6. | Summary: Eleven-year-old Sophia
endeavors to prevent her increasingly forgetful eighty-eight-year-old
neighbor and best friend Sophie from entering assisted living, and in
the process, uncovers unexpected stories of war, loss, and hope.
Identifiers: LCCN 2022045099 | ISBN 9780063299504 (hardcover)
Subjects: CYAC: Best friends—Fiction. | Friendship—Fiction.
| Dementia—Fiction. | Polish Americans—Fiction.
Classification: LCC PZ7.L9673 Tr 2024 | DDC [Fic]—dc23
LC record available at https://lccn.loc.gov/2022045099

Typography by Torborg Davern and Andrea Vandergrift
24 25 26 27 28 LBC 6 5 4 3 2

First Edition

For Maggie, Nancy, and Kay, in celebration
of friendship. And for all my friends of
the heart out there—and there are many—
who are seventy-seven years younger than I.

Tree.

Table.

Book.

CHAPTER

I

I am going to tell you three words. I'm choosing them at random. Listen carefully. This will be important.

House.

Umbrella.

Apple.

Remember those. I'll explain later.

CHAPTER

2

"One. Last night after dinner I threw up and eggplant came out of my nose," my friend Ralphie Mariani announced.

I pondered this. "Okay," I said. "Next."

"Two. My father was born in an Italian village on the side of a volcano and once there was ash all over his baby carriage."

"Yeah. Go on."

"Three. There was a huge spider in my sister's bedroom this morning and the cat grabbed it and ate it."

Easy peasy. "One," I told him. "One is a lie. That was so lame, Ralphie. I've heard about your father's volcano a zillion times. And everybody knows that Piccolina eats everything. Of course she would eat a spider. So the nose barf is the lie."

"Yeah, you're right," Ralphie said with a shrug. "I gotta think of better truths. Are we even now?"

"No. I'm way ahead, Ralphie. Eighteen to seven."

"You think I'm getting better?"

"Maybe a little. Keep working at it."

It's just this game we play: two truths and a lie. Ralphie is not very good at it. He is quite smart in school, actually—we're in the same class—but, well, I'll describe it this way: If you were to go down an alphabetical list of Ralphie's genetic markers, and you got to S in the alphabet? You would find a strong science gene, not surprising, because his dad is a doctor, and I think those things can be inherited. Then you would also find a gene for shortness, also probably inherited; Dr. Mariani is maybe five-six, shorter than my mother, and Ralphie is shorter than that, shorter than me. I think he has some growing time left, but he is not ever going to be a basketball star.

But you would find no gene for subtlety, not in Ralphie. And the two-truths-and-a-lie game requires some pretty subtle thinking.

The secret is to think of bizarre, unbelievable truths. Well, here: I'll give you an example.

One: I am going to be twelve on my next birthday, in September.

Two: My middle name is Henry, even though I am a girl.

Three: My best friend is seventy-seven years older than I am.

The lie is number one. My birthday was actually this month, a week ago, July 22 to be exact. I just turned eleven. But I bet you guessed one of the others, right? Because they both seem so weird and unbelievable.

But my name is Sophia Henry Winslow. My parents had sort of planned on a boy, and didn't get one, and the doctor told them: no more babies. So they gave me the Henry that they had planned on, and actually I kind of like it.

And it is also true about my best friend being eighty-eight years old. My best friend is named Sophie Gershowitz.

This story (a true one) is (mostly) about me and her.

CHAPTER

3

You know what? It's not that hard to write a story. You need all the obvious stuff: characters, setting, plot details (what happened, why it happened, what's going to happen next) and, of course, an ending. That's it, pretty much. Some kids in my class groan when we have a Creative Writing assignment. But not me. For me it's an easy A. I just put together all the ingredients as if I were making spaghetti sauce. If the recipe asks for herbs? I sprinkle in a few adverbs and adjectives. And that's it. That's how you write a story.

There are many ways to start.

Once upon a time.

It was a dark and stormy night.

"Where's Papa going with that ax?"

(To name a few.)

But I have been struggling a bit with how to start this one. An author once visited my school and talked about writing books. Kids asked a lot of questions. They asked how much money she makes, and does she have pets, and is she going to write another book. Her answers were: "Not enough, ha ha ha." And "Yes, a miniature poodle." And "Yes, I am." Pretty dull answers.

But then a kid asked what is the best way to start a book, and her answer was one that made me stop and think. She said, "Begin on the day that is different."

I suppose, in a way, she's right. One night Max puts on his wolf suit, makes mischief, and yikes—that's a different day for sure, and it's the start of *Where the Wild Things Are*. One day is different because it's the day that Mr. and Mrs. Mallard start looking for a place to live, and ta-da! You get *Make Way for Ducklings*. Each of those stories begins on a day that is different.

But isn't *every* day different? Even the most ordinary day is different from the one before. For example, on Sunday I wore flip-flops all day. But Sunday night, on *60 Minutes*, they talked about Lyme disease and it made me nervous, so yesterday, Monday, I wore sneakers and tucked the bottoms of my jeans into my socks, just to keep deer ticks from getting at me. So the day was a little different. (Also very hot.)

And today? Tuesday. An ordinary day. It didn't seem at all *different* except that I had just overheard a conversation that made me angry and worried. After that I started having a vague thought about the empty house across the street—a dilapidated house, shabby, actually a little scary, but one in which you could hide things. *Keep them safe*. And then, in part because of this very secret, very unnerving thought, the day became different. And so this particular story begins.

To start, I will tell you about the characters: the two people involved. There are others, of course. But the main ones are me and Sophie Gershowitz.

CHAPTER

4

Sophie Gershowitz is my next-door neighbor and my best friend. She's my first best friend, actually. I have plenty of acquaintances, and classmates, and when I was little I had playdates, but somehow I never seemed to acquire a true best friend, someone who understands my woes and shares my joys and laughs at the same things that I find funny. Not until I met Sophie Gershowitz. She and I have many things in common. For one thing, we have the same first name. A golden retriever down the street shares it as well, but I think that does not count.

I do know others with the same name. There are several Sophies at my school. (And Emmas! I'm so glad I'm not an Emma!) But none of them are special. None of them love me.

Sophie Gershowitz tells me that her original name was Shlomit. She came here from another country, Poland actually, and for a while, for complicated reasons, in Poland she became Zofia, and then eventually her name was Americanized when she arrived in this country. Probably a good thing. I believe she might have been bullied if her name continued to be Shlomit or Zofia.

There is a bar in New York called Sophie's and it has a billiards table, according to Yelp, but I have never been there. There is a book and movie named *Sophie's Choice*, which I have not read or seen. And there is a famous violinist named Anne-Sophie Mutter. I googled her because I google all Sophies, and I found a fact that is so delicious that I say it to myself under my breath frequently just because it makes me smile. The fact is this:

Anne-Sophie Mutter has a daughter named *Arabella Wunderlich*.

How I yearn for a name like that! But then, of course, I would not have the same name as my very dearest friend, Sophie Gershowitz.

I am seventy-seven years younger than Sophie Gershowitz, who is eighty-eight years old.

I could say *you do the math*, but why bother. I have already told you. I am eleven.

CHAPTER

5

I wanted to go right ahead to the various plot points and secondary characters: neighborhood, houses, teakettles, Ralphie, games, Oliver, and many others. But I know that when you are telling (or writing) a story, it helps to keep the audience interested if you insert action. So I am going to do that right now.

Action: I went into the kitchen a while ago and made myself a cheese sandwich. Then I dialed the phone. I knew the number by heart because I was calling Ralphie.

Oh, wait. I have to interrupt the action now by

explaining Ralphie. I have already *mentioned* Ralphie, I know, but now I am going to *explain* him.

Ralphie's family, which lives across the street, is the Mariani family, and they have six children. Sophie Gershowitz says that this is because they are of Italian descent. Italians have big families, she tells me, because they are Catholic and Catholics are supposed to have big families, apparently. We do not understand the reason for this. Sophie Gershowitz and I are somewhat dubious about Catholic rules, though of course we are respectful.

Ralphie has two older sisters—one in college, one in high school—and a brother in the army, and two little brothers in second and third grade. Also a cat, and some goldfish.

Dr. Mariani is a pediatrician so he probably likes children and maybe that is another reason, nothing to do with the Catholic church, that they have six. Also, he probably gets their vitamins for free.

Ralphie's mom is a fantastic cook. I am sad to say that my mother is not. My mother has a college degree hanging on the wall of her office but she thinks that canned tuna fish mixed with canned mushroom soup with canned onion rings on the top is a legitimate casserole. Don't get me wrong, I love my mom. But last Christmas I gave her an Ina Garten cookbook (which I got at the library's annual Gently Used Books Sale, but take my word for it, this book had never been opened—it was pristine) with a loving note from me about how I hoped she would enjoy thrilling her family with some of these recipes, especially the one for Chocolate Pecan Meringue Torte on page 183. Not a chance. She glanced at the picture but didn't even read the list of ingredients.

Mrs. Mariani, though! Different story altogether. Every now and then we have a neighborhood get-together—we did this on the Fourth of July, just a few weeks ago. I happen to have a chart depicting the Healthy Eating Pyramid on the wall of my bedroom. My fourth grade teacher was cleaning out her supply closet and planned to throw it away because it was out of date but she let me take it home. To be honest, I thought it had to do with Egypt ("Pyramid"—right? I hadn't looked at it carefully) and I was very interested in mummies at the time. Then when I realized my mistake, I actually examined it and found that food was almost as interesting as mummies. And since then I've become something of a nut about nutrition.

But I think holidays are an exception, and if you want to eat nothing but Peeps and chocolate bunnies on Easter, that's okay.

So: Fourth of July? Anything goes. Ralphie's mom made a huge lasagna, a giant salad with at least four different kinds of lettuce, and a six-layer cake with tiramisu between the layers. Our neighbor Margaret Voorhees brought homemade brownies, which her son Oliver had measured (Oliver loves to measure) and cut with such precision that each brownie was exactly one and a half by one and a half inches square. Sophie Gershowitz brought a Jell-O mousse (recipe in the local paper . . . okay, not that great, but people pretended that they liked it). Other people brought hot dogs and baked beans and potato salad but my mother was the only one who didn't cook stuff herself. My own mother contributed a pineapple upside-down cake that she bought at the supermarket.

But guess what: Ralphie loved it. He didn't even taste his mom's lasagna. He ate a hot dog half-heartedly and then four helpings of pineapple upside-down cake. As I told you, I think holidays can be a nutritional exception, but four pieces of pineapple upside-down cake, not even homemade? Come on. I whispered *junk food* to Ralphie several times, to no avail. And he drank a whole lot of Coke. His parents didn't even tell him to stop.

You would think that given his medical training, Dr. Mariani would advise his children carefully about their diet: green leafy vegetables, for example. Ralphie didn't even touch his mother's salad. I might put a leaflet on this topic through their mail slot, though perhaps that would be a little like an anonymous letter, and I do not approve of those.

Ralphie Mariani is my very close friend (not my best; Sophie Gershowitz is that) and he does very well in school, but he has insufficient knowledge about nutrition and also he is lacking in self-control.

(Everyone has self-control issues, of course. My father told me that once he found his favorite movie,

Lawrence of Arabia, on Netflix, and even though he'd already seen it three times in movie theaters, he watched it on Netflix, and then—here's where he went truly overboard—even though it was one a.m. and my mom had gone to bed two hours earlier, he went back to the beginning and watched it again.)

CHAPTER

6

So anyway: Back to Tuesday. I called Ralphie to ask a favor of him.

Explanation required here. It's a little embarrassing. But Ralphie and I are the only middle-school-age kids in this neighborhood. And a couple of years ago our parents got together and made a pact. I think Dr. Mariani is the one who came up with the idea because he read something in one of his zillion periodicals about children and the causes of their emotional problems. Anyway, he and his wife and my parents—the four of them, so Ralphie and I are totally outnumbered—agreed that we would not be allowed to have cell phones until we are twelve. *Do you believe that? Is that not completely irrational?* But they made their minds up (and by the way, made Ralphie and me the laughingstocks of our entire school . . . not that we weren't already).

Anyway. I dialed the Marianis' number.

We used to have certain telephone rituals we went through. He would say *"Moshi moshi,"* which is what Japanese people say when they answer the telephone. His parents made him to stop doing that because even though his father has a separate telephone for his medical practice, sometimes patients get panicky, like maybe if their child is unconscious, and call the Mariani family line by mistake and then they get all upset if someone answers in Japanese. (Okay, this has happened.) So now (most of the time, because occasionally he forgets and slips back into old habits) Ralphie answers the way he did yesterday. He said, "Mariani residence."

Then I said, *"Moshi moshi"* for old times' sake.

And he said, "Hi, Sophie."

(Sometimes conversation isn't too interesting but

in order to be completely accurate I am including the boring parts like "Hi, Sophie.")

Then we did the truth-and-lie thing, not for any reason, just because we usually do it. After that I got to the point.

I said, "I need the Merck."

And after a moment of not saying anything, Ralphie said, "Okay. What's two?"

"Ralphie, it's not two truths and a lie. We did that already."

"Oh. So you really need the Merck? You borrowed it last month."

"Yeah. I thought I might have schistosomiasis. I had an itchy rash."

"Well, that was poison ivy. I had it too. I think we got it in the backyard of the fixer-upper-for-sale house."

"I know that, Ralphie. But at first—until I checked the Merck—I thought it might be schistosomiasis. Only it turns out people can't get schistosomiasis in the United States. You have to travel to Africa or India."

"I'm never going to those places," Ralphie said.

"I might. But not till I'm older."

"Why do you need the Merck, then?"

"Other reasons," I told him. "Private."

Ralphie went silent for a minute. Then he said, in a low voice, "Please, please tell me you're not going to read about private parts."

I groaned. "No, Ralphie. I only meant that my reason for needing the Merck is a personal one. And I'm still mulling it over, actually. I'll explain it to you later."

"Oh. Good. Okay," Ralphie said. "I'll bring it over."

Next I will explain the Merck.

CHAPTER

7

If you are a doctor, you already know this and can skip this part. The Merck Manual is a book. It tells you absolutely everything you want to know about medical stuff. It can be somewhat frightening to read it. (But it is important to know these things. The right piece of information at the right time can save your life.)

It is also online, of course, like everything else in the world, and I have looked things up in the Merck on my computer, like once when I thought I might be suffering from a pyogenic granuloma because I had a sort of a zit on my nose.

The online Merck told me that the base of a pyogenic granuloma may be pedunculated and surrounded by a collarette of epidermis, which was more than I needed to know, and made me somewhat alarmed. While I was worrying, my zit disappeared.

And yes, I do have a laptop, even though I don't have a cell phone. So does Ralphie. We need them for school. But when our parents made the completely irrational rule about cell phones, they also instituted what they call the computer protocols. Our computers are in the public areas of our houses—living rooms, family rooms, occasionally okay to set them on the kitchen table—but not in our bedrooms. Our parents have to know all our passwords and we can't do secret stuff on our computers, cannot converse with strangers, *blah blah blah.* As if! (And by the way, guess who got scammed when he got an email saying his Amazon account had been frozen and he had to *click here* to update his info—my dad.)

Anyway, I could easily have opened the online Merck. But then my parents would have noticed what I was reading online, because they always look, even though I have never once given them any reason to be concerned. (Well, maybe once, when they saw that I was looking at the website of a Connecticut dog breeder who had Irish wolfhound puppies for sale.) Not that I was looking up anything subversive in the Merck. I just didn't want to discuss it with them.

And anyway, I want the book, the actual book, not the internet Merck, when I am feeling overwhelmed with anxiety about a medical situation. There is something about a book: the feel of it, the weight of it in your hands, the way the pages turn (pages in the Merck are very thin and extremely serious-seeming, the cover is leather, and there are built-in index tabs). And that is why I asked Ralphie to let me borrow it, after the very upsetting conversation I had overheard the day before.

CHAPTER

8

Just to be clear: I was not eavesdropping. I am completely against eavesdropping, except in the case of the FBI, maybe, listening in on spies.

And they were not whispering. It was all very up front and matter-of-fact. I was on the floor in the living room, using the coffee table as a kind of desk and thinking about writing a thank-you note, which my mother had insisted I should do, to my great-aunt, who had sent me a disgusting birthday gift. They were in the kitchen, one room away, talking about a phone call from Aaron, Sophie Gershowitz's son.

My father: "Aaron Gershon's coming to visit his mother on Friday."

My mother: "How do you know that?"

My father: "He called me at the office. I offered to pick him up at the Manchester airport but he said no, he's flying into Boston and renting a car."

My mother: "How long is he staying? I'll invite him and his mother over for dinner."

My father: "Uncertain. He's meeting with her doctor on Saturday. So he'll be here over the weekend at least. Maybe longer, depending on what the doctor says."

My mother: "Goodness, she isn't sick, is she? I saw her sweeping the back porch this morning and she looked just fine."

My father: "No, it's the usual problem. Getting worse, Aaron says."

My mother: "He should take her to live with him in Akron."

My father: "With that wife of his?"

Laughter from both.

CHAPTER

9

So . . . you're wondering why that conversation was so upsetting?

Sorry. I made myself laugh there for a minute because I was using Sophie Gershowitz's voice. She begins sentences with "so" (and often follows that with "my darling").

Explanation. My parents were talking about my best friend, and they were using phrases like "usual problem" and "getting worse." It is upsetting when such phrases are used in connection with friendships.

First, a word about friendships. The problem is

that people have a wrong impression of friendships, especially when they involve sixth grade girls, like me. (Actually, full disclosure: I just finished fifth grade, am going into sixth.) People right away start thinking of giggling, and writing notes to each other, and texting, and probably talking about clothes, and music, and which boys they like.

None of that is true friendship. It is only *practice*.

Sophie Gershowitz and I have a true and lasting friendship, a friendship of the heart. It began, actually, when I was nine.

I had just gotten, that September, two things: braces on my teeth, and glasses. I needed both, it is true. My teeth were crooked and the orthodontist, in addition to my parents, had assured me that after my malocclusion (a horrible word, but it is the official word for crooked teeth) was corrected—which would take several years—they would be perfect and I would be beautiful.

As for the glasses? It was nice to be able to see. The world took me by surprise. I had assumed everyone saw trees as big blurs of green (starting to be red and orange, actually; the foliage was early, that fall) but suddenly, after they did vision tests in school and my parents got a note marked URGENT, and they took me to an eye doctor? Now I could see actual individual *leaves*. But the plaid frames I had chosen, when I got my glasses, turned out to be uncool. Apparently, there was a very dorky character in Saturday morning cartoons who wore exactly the same glasses. But I never watch cartoons. Who knew?

So, three things: one, the braces, which made me lisp so that when I said "yes" it sounded like "yeth" for a while until my tongue got used to things. (Back then I would have said "youthed to thingths.") Two, the plaid plastic eyeglass frames, which made me look like a cartoon person everyone laughed at. And three? Well, I did a dumb thing. This was right at the time when I had begun to be interested in nutrition, and I started thinking about the lunches in the school cafeteria, and okay, I went overboard and made a big poster suggesting that they stop serving macaroni and cheese, spaghetti, and pizza, because there were way too many carbs for growing kids and we should have green leafy vegetables. I suggested brussels sprouts and spinach. And of course, I was suddenly not only unpopular but something of a laughingstock. Not that I had ever been Miss Congeniality or anything, but I had always had friends at school.

And now I didn't. Girls who had come to my birthday party that summer—and who had liked me then—now turned mean and made fun of me. Boys said "Ewww" when they were assigned to be my partner for projects—dumb stuff, like making a volcano in science class. Who cared? And when the teacher divvied us up into pairs and someone got *me*, it was like last prize (unless it was Ralphie, who always stayed my friend, but he was also unpopular, so it didn't count).

Then one Saturday afternoon my parents abandoned me too.

It was a mistake, of course.

My father was driving to Manchester to pick up some brochures from the printer's, and he had asked if I wanted to go with him, and I hadn't made up my mind yet.

But my mom thought I had gone. She took off on some errands, to the garden center to get some shrubs to beef up the yard, and after that she was heading to Concord, where there was a terrific bookstore that *of course* I would like to go to—but she went without me because she thought I'd gone with my dad.

But my dad had left and thought I was with her.

Instead I was over at Ralphie's house. He and I had been inventing a board game. We had it all laid out on a card table we'd set up in his living room. It was a complicated game, and we spent a lot of time arguing over whether it was against the law to use things, like *Get Out of Jail Free*, that Monopoly had already used. His two little brothers were running around throwing Legos at each other, which was annoying.

And by the time I got home, both of my parents—each of them thinking I was with the other—were gone and the front door was locked, and I went around and tried the back door and it was locked too. I could have gone back to Ralphie's house, of course. But we had not parted amicably. Actually, to be honest, I had said as I left, "Why don't you just throw the whole game away, Ralphie, because nobody's going to want to play it if it's just a copy of every game they've already played a thousand times!" And he sort of slammed the door behind me.

And on top of that my teeth ached because the orthodontist had tightened my braces the day before, and my glasses still had hideous plaid frames, and clearly no one liked me, not Ralphie and not even my parents, and so I did what any mature and intelligent person would do: I sat down on the back steps of my house and burst into tears.

Next thing I knew, the old lady next door—who had lived there all my life but although I knew her name I had never paid her the slightest bit of attention—noticed me from her porch, and came scurrying across her backyard, opened the gate in the fence, and stood looking briefly at me, then sat down beside me on the step, opened up her arms, and said, "My darling girl, my darling girl." And I sank right in against her (rather large) chest, knocking my ugly glasses sideways, and I sobbed that I had no home anymore because my parents had abandoned me, and she didn't laugh. She took a crumpled tissue out of the pocket of her apron and wiped the snot off my upper lip, and she just listened, rocking me back and forth, saying, "I know, I know just how it feels." She took me to her house, to her kitchen, and gave us each a glass of kiwi strawberry water. Then she told me a really dumb joke about a horse who goes into a bar and the bartender says *Why the long face?* and my own long face gradually disappeared into a giggling face and before the day was over she was my very best friend and has remained so ever since.

CHAPTER

10

Sophie Gershowitz and I love and loathe the same things. Love: banana bread, otters, the color mauve (mauve is a sort of purple, actually), the Statue of Liberty, and the composer Prokofiev. Prokofiev wrote "Peter and the Wolf," but that is not his best work. We like to listen to Prokofiev's Classical Symphony. Sophie Gershowitz has old records and a turntable. We put the Classical Symphony on and then we direct with our hands, and we listen for the part in the first movement that is so hard for the violins that we always get tensed up, wondering if one will get it wrong, but they never do. We hum some parts.

Loathe: North Korea, reality TV, animal abuse, and stewed rhubarb.

We feel blasé (*blasé* is a word I love. I am going to make a list of words I love, probably soon) about—let me think—*People* magazine, Broadway musicals (not that I have ever been to one), oboes and bassoons, and quesadillas.

Also, Sophie Gershowitz and I are the only two people in this entire town who know how to play a card game called Zioncheck. She taught me.

We love her cat, Mr. Katz, who is quite elderly and very aloof and pretends not to love us back (but we can see through that; he actually adores us both). And we both still mourn his sibling, Catsy, who one day this past spring wandered off into the bushes at the back of the yard and never reappeared. We looked and looked for her, calling her name, but . . . *nothing.*

"She was very old," Sophie Gershowitz pointed out. "You know what I think? She knew her time was coming to an end, and she didn't want to bother us—or Mr. Katz, even though he is her brother—about it. So she looked for a private place and went there. A place where no one would intrude on her. Cats do that. Maybe dogs, too, but I don't know much about dogs."

"But Catsy might be in pain!" I said. "And hungry, or lonely!"

"I don't think so, my darling. I think she wanted not to be bothered by people fussing with her. She just wanted to lie quietly and enjoy the solitude and watch the night come."

"Maybe," I replied, a little dubious.

Now and then, still, I find myself poking at the bushes where we last saw Catsy—lifting a branch thick with leaves, and looking behind it, as if she might be there. But of course she is not, and won't be, ever. Sometimes, when we are having a cool drink of kiwi strawberry water, Sophie Gershowitz and I clink our glasses together and say "To Catsy," as a remembrance and as a reminder to ourselves that we shouldn't be sad because it is Nature's Way.

Sophie Gershowitz has taught me many things. Teaches, I mean. Present tense. I am still learning from her. And I think that learning from each other is one of the most important parts of friendship.

CHAPTER

11

have started keeping a list of words that I despise.

Vermin.

Torso.

Malocclusion.

CHAPTER

12

You can zoom in on my New Hampshire small-town neighborhood with Google Earth and you will see the street I live on. I prefer curved and winding roads. They make me think about Stuart Little setting off in his tiny car to look for love. But you can't choose where you are born, and I was born here. Actually, I was born in a regional hospital. And then I was brought home, wearing a yellow onesie, to this short, straight, dead-end street called Chocorua Street. (I will tell you more about the street name later.)

But for now, I will describe my neighborhood.

There are eight houses altogether and the houses are not new. There are no split-levels, no ranch styles, no low-slung modern houses such as you might find in California or on the cover of *Architectural Digest*. And no antiques, either: no widow's walks, no pillars.

Just ordinary, somewhat old-fashioned two-story houses, like ones you might read about in, oh, maybe old-fashioned books about Ramona Quimby or Nancy Drew. Most have front porches. Some are bigger than others. Mine is average, and in the middle of the block. I won't describe my family yet; that will be later. (And won't take long. We are dull.)

On one side of us is Sophie Gershowitz's house. She has lived there for many, many years—most of them with her husband and son. But her husband died ages ago. Aaron, her son (soon to visit, also topic of recent unsettling overheard conversation), has grown up and married and moved away, and now she lives there alone.

I will not bore you with a description of the others, but that is my side of Chocorua Street: five houses, all commonplace. Opposite, across the street, only three. One is the Marianis'.

Next door to the Mariani family and directly across the street from mine is an empty house. You can barely see it because of the overgrown trees and bushes. It is For Sale. There is a sign in the yard, and every two weeks a man comes from the real estate agency and mows the small patch of lawn.

Every now and then there is an ad in the local paper for the For Sale house. It says things like "Handyman's delight" or "Fixer-upper" or "Needs TLC" (tender loving care, my mother explained, because I didn't recognize the abbreviation). But still, it doesn't sell. I think the ad should be honest and say, "You can get this house cheap because it is falling apart and looks a little scary." But no one asked me.

I have looked through the windows from the front porch (this is not considered trespassing when a house is For Sale) and I can see that the living room wallpaper (pale green, with vague leaf shapes) is badly stained from leaks around the windows. From the porch windows I can only glimpse the kitchen slightly through a partly opened door, but I can see enough to know that the stove should definitely be replaced, and the kitchen floor is an ugly linoleum, very discolored and scuffed.

The people who once lived there moved to a fancier neighborhood after they inherited some money from the wife's father. (This is common knowledge, not gossip. Sophie Gershowitz and I are very much opposed to gossip.)

It has been empty for months now. The tree branches hang over the front porch and shadow everything, and there are vines growing on the railings. Flakes of dry old paint drift onto the overgrown bushes and are held there until spattering rain dislodges them.

Altogether it is a house that seems to *need* something. I have been thinking a lot lately about the fixer-upper house and its possibilities. These are somewhat scary thoughts, so I am not going to divulge them.

I'll go on in my description to finally the last house on the street, the one on the other side of the Marianis. It belongs to a single mother. Her name is Margaret Voorhees, and she works as a hostess at the Chocorua Steak House. Day shift, usually, unless someone doesn't show up and she has to stay over. Her little boy is named Oliver. He is seven and—and—well, I don't quite know how to describe Oliver, except to say that he is an *unusual* boy.

We do not know anything at all about Oliver's father. But Margaret Voorhees is an attentive mother and when she is not at work, she does a lot of educational things with Oliver: nature walks, library visits, tae kwon do classes. He is getting better at eye contact lately and Margaret thinks tae kwon do has done that for him.

Oliver could read when he was two and a half years old. I am not kidding. The first thing I heard him read was *Goodnight Moon* and I thought he had memorized it the way little kids do when someone has read a book to them many times. So I tested him. I picked a random book out of a stack and opened it in the middle. Oliver looked at the page and read, "The caterpillar ate through one nice green leaf . . ." Then he stopped, looked solemnly at the page for a moment, and turned to me and said, "*Caterpillar* is a hard word because it has four syllables."

So, there you have it. Oliver Voorhees is unique.

He is in the category of *friend*, along with Ralphie Mariani and Sophie Gershowitz. But he is a special kind of friend, not one like Ralphie with whom you play two truths and a lie, which would be very very confusing for Oliver, who only tells truths, always. And not one with whom you would plan complicated undertakings and adventures; that would also be Ralphie. Also, not really a Friend of the Heart—that is Sophie Gershowitz, of course.

Let me think. Oliver is a friend whom you don't exactly understand but whom you love and appreciate anyway.

(Did you notice that I just said *whom* four times in a row? Grammar is of interest to me. My fifth-grade English teacher, Mr. Rohrbaugh, was an expert at grammar and really got me going with *whom*s. I don't count Mr. Rohrbaugh as a friend. I would never call him by his first name, for example—his first name is Harold—and I know nothing about his lifestyle or what kind of car he drives or his favorite food. You would know those details about a friend, for example Sophie Gershowitz, who drives an ancient Oldsmobile and whose favorite food is a Reuben sandwich.

Still, I will be forever grateful to Harold Rohrbaugh for instilling me with *whom*s, and also making clear the difference between *lay* and *lie*, something that too many people, even very smart people—Ralphie, for example—get wrong. Ralphie again and again says, "So I was laying on the couch—" and when I interrupt him to say "*Lying*, Ralphie" he thinks we are playing the game again and says, "No, no, I really was laying on the couch—" and then I just sigh and give up. Let someone else teach him proper grammar. I hope he marries an English teacher someday.)

13

I am not going to dwell on this because what purpose would that serve? But I did say that I would discuss the name of our street. Chocorua is a Native American word, and the name of a New Hampshire mountain, and supposedly it was the name of a Native American man who lived in the Tamworth Valley in the 1700s.

The story goes that Chocorua became angry at some settlers (probably, in my opinion, with good reason) and put a curse on all white men.

Here is the curse: *"May the Great Spirit curse*

you when he speaks in the clouds and his words are fire! Lightning blast your crops! Wind and fire destroy your homes! The Evil One breathe death on your cattle! Panthers howl and wolves fatten on your bones!"

As curses go, I think this is a really terrifying one and it makes me wonder whether it was wise to name a street after the guy who first said it.

But, as I said, I am not going to dwell on it. I do, however, dwell on Chocorua Street.

CHAPTER

14

Remember this overheard (not eavesdropped on) conversation?

> *My father: "Aaron Gershon's coming to visit*
> *his mother on Friday."*
> *My mother: "How do you know that?"*

Aaron Gershon changed his last name when he became an accountant—for business purposes, he told his mother. "Funny business," Sophie Gershowitz said when she told me about it, and rolled her eyes.

Aaron is an accountant, and there is nothing whatsoever funny about being an accountant, except for this saying:

Aaron the Accountant from Akron is an Annoyance.

That is not a well-known saying, not something you would find in one of my favorite books, the book called *Bartlett's Quotations*. It is simply part of a game that Sophie Gershowitz and I play from time to time, a game we made up that keeps us amused.

It started with Aaron, actually, but the rest of it is imaginary people. Here are a few that we have made up:

Bill the Bartender from Boston is a Bully.

Edna the EMT from Easthampton is an Extrovert.

Caroline the Comedian from Charleston is a Character.

There are others but I don't see the need to list them all, because you get the idea. We create these people, Sophie Gershowitz and I, and then we marry them to each other (we even have a same-sex couple, Harry from Hoboken, who is married to Will from

Wichita. They're hoping to have a child, and their surrogate, who lives in Seattle, is named Suzanne) and make up stories about their lives. It whiles away the time.

Being eighty-eight, Sophie Gershowitz does not have a lot of outside activities. I could have outside activities if I wanted to—my mother keeps urging me to take up a hobby; she suggests origami, or scrap-booking—but I prefer to spend my spare time with my best friend, sitting in her kitchen sipping tea or vitamin water (we both prefer the kiwi strawberry) and thinking up games like the one I just described. I found myself hoping that Aaron Gershon, who is arriving Friday, was not going to stay too long because he is an Interruption and also, as his mother says, something of an *Annoyance*, and who would know better than his own mother.

Aaron, who, as you know, lives in Akron, doesn't call his mother as often as she would like. He wants his mother to learn to do email but she isn't inter-ested. Sometimes he comes to visit but by the time he leaves she always says his visit was one day too long and he uses the word *should* too often. She should get a computer. She should hire a cleaning lady. She should balance her checkbook. She should move to Akron.

Move to Akron?! She and I were shocked that he even suggested it. She has lived here her whole adult life. She came to this country when she was eighteen, met Max Gershowitz (slightly older, probably seemed glamorous and alluring), married him a couple of years later, and moved with him into the very house where she now lives, after their marriage sixty-eight years ago. Aaron was born in this house. When he was nine, he tripped on an untied shoelace (she had told him and *told him* to tie his shoe), fell down the stairs in this house, and chipped a front tooth. His Boy Scout uniform is still hanging in the closet of his old bedroom in this house. Sophie's husband, Max (the newspaper obituary, which she has shown me, calls her *the love of his life*, in the part that starts "survived by"), died many years ago, right in the bedroom with yellow flowered wallpaper at the top of the stairs. I'd like to say she was holding his hand at the moment of his death, but actually she was lying next to him sound asleep and didn't even know until she woke up in the morning and discovered that he had not.

There are memories and mementos in her house that are the story of her life. How could she possibly leave them behind? Not to mention her leaving her very best friend?

D*** it all!

Sorry. I am against profanity as a rule. And I have used asterisks so it is only semi-profanity. But I just get so upset, thinking about it, that Aaron would want his mother to move away. May lightning blast his crops!

CHAPTER

15

And now it is worse. Now he is going to use force. Or invoke the law, which is pretty much the same thing. I know this because my parents told me, when I explained that I had overheard their conversation and asked what the heck was going on.

"Sweetie," my mother said, "Mrs. Gershowitz is becoming very forgetful."

I laughed. "Like you!" I told her. "Like the other day when you went grocery shopping and forgot to get paper towels even though it was right there on the list!"

My mom gave me a rueful look. "Yeah, that was silly," she said.

"Not really," I said. "Everybody forgets stuff. Like just last night I meant to watch *Jeopardy!* because that woman was getting close to half a million dollars, but darn; I forgot to turn it on. She lost, though. I checked online."

My dad was listening. "This is a different kind of forgetful, Soph," he said. "This is called dementia."

"Early stages," my mother said hastily. "But Aaron's very concerned about her."

"What on earth are you talking about? *Dementia?* She's smarter than you and me put together! She knows all the words to every song that Frank Sinatra ever sang! She can tell you last year's Red Sox lineup! And also she can knit complicated patterns with more than one color! Sophie Gershowitz is probably the smartest person I know! She speaks Polish and German and English and—"

My father interrupted me. "It's her short-term memory," he explained. "Things from the past will stay with her longer. But the short-term memory goes first. Aaron's afraid that—"

Okay, I did a babyish thing. I put my hands over my ears and said "*La-la-la*" very loudly. My parents rolled their eyes, which in my opinion is a somewhat babyish reaction.

This conversation had taken place at noon on Monday after I overheard them talking about Aaron's phone call. My *la-la-la* reaction put an end to any discussion, as *la-la-la*s always do. But I had been thinking about it all afternoon. Then it was evening and we had just finished dinner. My mom started clearing the plates. I could see that my dad was glancing toward the TV and I knew he was going to turn on the evening news in a minute. They always watch *News Hour* together.

I put our forks into the dishwasher. "So what exactly is Aaron going to do?" I asked, trying to use a casual-sounding voice. "Send guys in white suits to put her in a straitjacket and haul her away? What's the plan here? Just so I'm prepared. Clue me in."

"Good heavens," my mother said. "Of course not. Aaron's arranged to have her tested. There are tests that doctors do, of cognition. What happens next will be determined by how she does on the tests.

There will be options. He's thinking assisted living, maybe. There's a place near him in Akron. Or—"

I stopped listening. I didn't need to know the options. Not when I heard the word *tests*. Now, that is something a person can deal with. Me, I am terrific at tests.

The only thing that tests require are study, and practice. Piece of cake. I could handle this. This was why I called Ralphie today about borrowing the Merck. To prepare.

CHAPTER

16

update all my lists frequently. Here is:

Words I despise, Part 2:

Vermin

Torso

Malocclusion

Dementia

Impairment

Cognition

Vermin and *torso* are self-evident (*self-evident*

is a hyphenated word I learned from reading the Declaration of Independence). Everybody hates *vermin*.

And *torso* has gotten a pretty grim reputation ever since CSI shows became popular on television.

Malocclusion. Nothing to be said. My orthodontist says that my malocclusion is not as bad as some that he has seen. I consider that a backhanded compliment.

But I added *dementia* after the conversation with my parents, and *impairment* and *cognition* after leafing through the Merck. This is what I had read:

> *Examination of mental status is done on anyone with an altered mental status or evolving impairment of cognition whether acute or chronic.*

I did not for one minute believe that Sophie Gershowitz's cognition was impaired. But if her son believed that, and if he was convincing my parents to believe that, then I decided I would do the work to prove them wrong. I would examine her mental status, using *tests*, using the Merck Manual instructions. It sounded pretty easy.

CHAPTER

17

There is another word that means "parents." *Progenitors.* You can also use it for grandparents, or great-grandparents, or even further back. It means those who came before.

My progenitors are named Eliot and Celia. Eliot and Celia met in college and they dated each other, though sometimes they had fights and dated other people for a while. Celia, whose last name at the time was McKittrick, once dated a guy named Julian—I forget his last name—who went on to become a congressman from some vowel state: Idaho, or Ohio, or

Iowa, something like that. He took her to a football game and then completely disregarded the fact that her feet got very cold. She had to stay for the whole game because Julian Whatever was a serious football fan. She could have gotten frostbite and had to have her toes amputated. He didn't even care.

Celia went back to Eliot after that. They didn't remember what they had fought about. After a while they graduated from college and got married. She took his last name, Winslow, and became Celia Winslow, and promised to love and honor him, which she has done, and he has also done, in reverse. She has also worked as his secretary, a good thing, if you ask me, because my male progenitor is somewhat disorganized. Celia keeps everything neatly filed; she is good at alphabetizing.

The name of my progenitors' company is Winslow Real Estate. When I mentioned earlier that a guy from the real estate office comes and mows the lawn of the scary abandoned house across the street? It was not really a lie, but it did conceal the truth. It is actually Eliot Winslow, my father, who mows. Every other week, in summer, he closes up the office and comes home a little early, changes into work pants and an old plaid shirt, and pushes the lawn mower across the street to tidy up the grass there, just in case someone wants to see the house. No one ever does, but he remains hopeful.

It is not difficult for him, coming home, because the office is attached to our house. It connects the house to the garage. Once it was called a breezeway, but then carpenters came and put up paneled walls. A rug person laid dark blue carpeting and two desks were delivered. A separate phone line was installed, and the breezeway turned into Winslow Real Estate. It was not illegal to do this. My father checked first with the zoning board. As long as he has only a small, tasteful sign—no neon—he can have his office here on Chocorua Street.

Celia and Eliot had hoped to have a large family. Many children. They had picked out names for both boys and girls. When their first child was a girl, they used the first girl name on their list—and also, as I explained, the first boy name too, and I became Sophia Henry Winslow. It does, I think, have a certain ring to it.

Unfortunately, other new parents at that time had chosen the same first name. As I mentioned, there are other Sophias at my middle school. I call myself Sophie and so do two others, but one of those spells it Sofie. And one uses the nickname Fee.

(There are seven Emmas.)

Sophie Gershowitz was not the only child in her family. She had a sister and several brothers. But, sadly, she is the only one remaining. I do not know what happened to the others. Old age, I guess.

CHAPTER

18

On Wednesday morning, I fixed myself a bowl of cornflakes with sliced banana, and while I was eating, I read the list, in my mother's handwriting, that was attached to the refrigerator by a small magnet shaped like a sailboat. (My parents were already at the office. I am allowed to go into the office, but I rarely do. It is boring there.) The list had to do with my obligations for the day. That is my mother's word, *obligations*.

July 27:

-Empty dishwasher.
-Practice piano.
-Fold laundry and take upstairs.
-Write thank-you note to Great-Aunt Kate.
PLEASE DO THIS!
-Ralphie called, wants you to call back.

This list was not bad, as my mother's lists go. I empty the dishwasher every day, have since I was eight. Same with laundry. She meant just my laundry—she does hers and Dad's. Piano practice? I hate it, but I do it. Actually, my mother said I could quit piano lessons if I want. But I am sticking with it just in case I ever decide that I want to be popular. Right now I don't much care. But just in case? I am on Book Four.

Thank-you note: Yeah, of course, what else is new. My birthday was three weeks ago. I have written to my grandparents (blouse, ugly) and my aunt and uncle (book, babyish) and I still have Great-Aunt Kate to do. She sent me bath salts. I do not even know what to do with bath salts. I read some-where that you can get a urinary tract infection from putting additives in your bathwater. I am not going to risk it. I only take showers.

And Ralphie? I decided I'd call him later. He's only probably going to complain about something wrong with his computer. Or that he doesn't know how to install something. I'll have to go over and do it for him, or reboot the whole thing because he screwed something up, and my parents say I am not allowed to charge him anything. So Ralphie can wait.

Dear Great-Aunt Kate,

*Thank you very much for the bath
salts. I have never had bath salts before.
In fact, I have never had any kind of
bathwater additive. Isn't it interesting that
they call them salts? What if they called
them bath peppers? Ha ha. Seriously,
the container is very pretty, and lemon
verbena is one of my favorite scents. Well,
lemon is. I have not smelled verbena*

before. But I expect I will like it very
much.

Love,
Sophie

There. Done. I left it on the kitchen table so that my mother could write the address, which I do not know, and add a stamp, which I do not have.

I emptied the dishwasher and then added my cereal bowl and spoon so that it was no longer empty. I decided to fold the laundry later. Piano practice could wait as well. Right now, ten a.m., I wanted to go next door and visit Sophie Gershowitz. I wanted to find out if she knew that her son was coming to visit, and how she felt about it if she did.

CHAPTER

19

Her house smelled a little odd this morning. To be honest, it often does. When you start getting old, some of your faculties start to diminish. Sophie Gershowitz is lucky. She can still hear just fine, and with her glasses on (sometimes she misplaces them—once she panicked and kept saying, "My glasses! I can't find my glasses!" and it turned out they were right there, perched on top of her head), she can see perfectly. Every year now they test her eyesight and every year they renew her driver's license.

But I'm afraid maybe her sense of smell has gotten a little uncertain. I have taken it upon myself to look through her refrigerator every couple of days and throw away anything that has turned bad. Sometimes there is a forgotten cucumber, squishy and liquefying, or occasionally a lemon with a gray-green fuzz. Milk can be a problem. Sophie Gershowitz likes milk in her tea, but she buys half-gallon containers to be thrifty, and she keeps them too long and doesn't notice. One sniff, though, and I can tell.

Today it wasn't a food smell. Something had burned. There was a bit of smoky haze, still, in the air of her kitchen, and when I came through the back door, Sophie Gershowitz waved her arms about apologetically as if she could magically clear the air.

"Only you, my darling," she said. "I was afraid it was the fire department!"

I could see right away what had happened. She had turned on the burner under her teakettle. She had done it a thousand times before. But then she had gone off to do something else. Maybe she had been upstairs, or maybe she was out on the back porch calling her cat, Mr. Katz, and got distracted looking at the zinnias, which are blooming by her back fence. It's pretty easy to be distracted by zinnias.

Her teakettle water had boiled away, and after a while the kettle itself had become so hot that it had kind of melted. The bottom was charred black and the plastic handle was misshapen. A potholder lying in the sink beside the stove was blackened as well. I think she had used it to grab the teakettle and it may have caught fire. It made me nervous, seeing it. Good thing she threw it in the sink.

It was scary. But it could happen to anybody. I told her that.

"Could happen to anybody," I said. "I think my mom has done the same thing."

Sophie Gershowitz nodded. She looked at the ruined kettle. "I don't think it was made in the USA," she said. "They make things so cheap in other countries. Some of them use child labor, did you know that?"

"I'll put it in the trash for you after it cools off."

"Probably six-year-olds made that kettle and they didn't even get paid. It's shocking."

I seriously doubted whether six-year-olds would know how to make a kettle. But I put on my "I am shocked" expression (hands over ears, eyes wide, mouth in a very big O), which I had perfected after looking at a picture of a painting called *The Scream* by Edvard Munch. And that made Sophie Gershowitz do the same, and we looked "I am shocked" at each other until we both started to laugh.

She sat down at the table. I left the kitchen door open to air out the fumes of the melted plastic handle, and I came and sat with her.

"List of Things That Make You Feel Like You Screwed Up," I announced. Sophie Gershowitz likes my lists. She chuckled.

"You go first," she said.

"When you don't notice the sliding door to the deck is closed, and you walk right into the glass and whack your forehead," I said. I had done that last week.

She was silent. "Now you," I said.

She looked blank.

"How about when you can't find your glasses and

look everywhere, then it turns out they are on top of your head?"

Sophie Gershowitz chuckled. "Yes. That one."

"Now me. When you come out the girls' bathroom and don't realize that there is a piece of toilet paper stuck to your shoe, but of course everyone else notices it right away."

"You're a good girl," she said suddenly, and patted my hand.

"Thank you. It's your turn."

"My turn?"

"Our list. Stupid stuff. How about when you forget that you turned on the stove and you burn up the stupid teakettle?"

Sophie Gershowitz looked where I pointed, at the ruined teakettle in the sink. She nodded, but she didn't laugh. She looked sad.

"List of Bad Smells," I announced, to cheer her up. "Me first: burned plastic."

She smiled. "Litter box." She looked over at the little braided rug under the window, where Mr. Katz was snoozing.

I pondered. "Poopy diapers," I suggested.

"I remember those," Sophie Gershowitz said.

"How long has it been since you changed diapers?" I asked her. "How old is Aaron? He's about to retire, so: sixty, maybe? And they were cloth diapers, then, right? You had to wash them."

Sophie Gershowitz nodded. "I hung them on the clothesline. Or inside, if the weather was bad.

"What day is it?" she asked, suddenly.

"Wednesday."

"Aaron's coming on Friday," she told me.

So she knew.

CHAPTER

20

*Patients should be told that recording of
mental status is routine and that they should
not be embarrassed by its being done.*

"Now I am going to do something routine,"
I told Sophie Gershowitz as I took out the
Merck, with the right pages bookmarked, and my
notebook. We had brought in all the laundry from
the clothesline and folded it. She has a dryer, but
she will only use it in the winter when it's too icy or
windy to go out in the yard. She likes the smell of
fresh air on her clothes. I agree with her.

"You should not be embarrassed by this," I added.

"Embarrassed? When was I last embarrassed? In
1961, that's when."

"What happened in 1961?" If I asked Oliver Voorhees this question, he would list world events. Honestly, he can do that. I've tested him. I chose a year at random. I picked 1959, and Oliver thought for a moment and then said, "Alaska and Hawaii became states."

But when I asked Sophie Gershowitz what happened in 1961, she just laughed and said, "You think I'm going to tell you? It was embarrassing!"

"Come on. Please? I won't laugh."

"Oh, all right. Aaron was a baby. I was nursing him. Doorbell rang. I got up and went to the door with my blouse all open. Just wasn't thinking. It was Mormon missionaries. Nice young men. Wearing neckties! But they got all flustered, made me all flustered, Aaron started screaming. I just shut the door on them. Rude. But I was embarrassed."

"But you haven't been embarrassed since? Not ever?"

She wrinkled her forehead, thinking. Then she said, "No."

I couldn't help thinking how lucky she was. I am embarrassed at least three times every day. More than that during the school year.

"Okay, then," I told her. "In that case you definitely should not be embarrassed by this. It's routine."

I picked up my pencil, and then I checked the directions one more time.

1. Orientation.
Test the 3 parameters of orientation:
Person (What is your name?)
Time (What is today's date?)
Place (What is the name of this place?)

"What is your name?" I asked her.

She frowned at me as if I had turned stupid. But she answered. "Sophie Gershowitz."

"What is today's date?"

She shrugged and then glanced through the open kitchen window. "Hot." Then she noticed the newspaper there on the table and looked at it slyly. "July twenty-eight," she announced, reading the date.

Is that cheating, to look at the newspaper? Who am I to judge? "Correct. And last: What is the name of this place?"

Sophie squinted at me, puzzled. "It's the kitchen," she said.

She was right; it's a confusing question. "What is your address?" I asked her.

"Is this some kind of test?"

"Sort of," I told her. "Actually, it is. But don't feel embarrassed. It's routine. What is your address?"

She pointed to an envelope lying beside the newspaper. Her electric bill, unopened. "Twenty-One Chocorua Street," she read aloud, and looked triumphant. "What's my prize? Do I win the lottery?"

In my notebook, I put a check mark after Question 1. *Orientation.* She had passed Question 1 with flying colors. Piece of cake.

We went on to Question 2.

CHAPTER

21

*R*ing. *Ring.* Phone. My kitchen. I was back home, making myself a sandwich, after reminding Sophie Gershowitz to keep an eye on her Chunky soup—she always has Chunky soup for lunch— while it was heating on the stove.

She should get a microwave. Aaron has told her that a million times, but she says no. She doesn't understand microwaves, doesn't trust microwaves, is maybe actually afraid of microwaves. She heard someplace that it could explode your heart if you stand too close. I think she actually heard something about pacemakers (which, incidentally, Sophie Ger-showitz calls "peacemakers"), but she doesn't want to discuss it. It is one of the few things we disagree on.

Anyway: *Ring. Ring.*

"*Cześć?*" I should have said "Winslow Real Estate." (I am supposed to answer that way in case someone is moving here from Los Angeles and is looking to buy a McMansion. That has never once happened. But my father says it could.) But instead I said *hello* in Polish. Sophie Gershowitz taught me to say it a couple of years ago, and I haven't really gotten the hang of it, because you have to do weird things with your tongue. Polish babies learn to do that, but if you are nine years old, as I was, when you try for the first time, it is hard. It's still hard, two years later. I do like to answer the phone this way, though. It confuses people.

"Hi. It's Ralphie."

Well, it confuses everyone but Ralphie Mariani. He's used to it. I am going to learn how to say hello in Arabic, I think. Or maybe Basque.

"Hi, Ralphie. What's up?"

"Your mom said she'd tell you to call me."

I glanced at the note she had left. It was the fifth item. "Yeah, she told me. I just hadn't gotten to it yet."

"It was at least two and a half hours ago that I called."

"So? I wasn't up yet when you called, and after I got up, I had to go see Sophie Gershowitz."

"Why?" Sometimes Ralphie seems to have no social skills whatsoever. His *why* was very intrusive because it was really none of Ralphie's business *why*. I answered him anyway.

"Because she's my friend, and she's old and needs checking on. Duh."

"Is she okay?"

"Yeah. But she melted her teakettle. I told her I'd go with her to Walmart to buy a new one. You want to come?"

"In her car?"

"Of *course* in her car. You think we're going to call an Uber or something, to go to stupid Walmart?"

"My dad says she shouldn't be driving."

I groaned. "Her eyesight is totally correctable and she can see as well as anybody when she has her glasses on. Which she always does, unless she's asleep!"

"He wasn't talking about her eyesight," Ralphie said. "It's her mental condition. Actually, he said her cognition, and I didn't know what that meant—"

"That's a horrible word. It's on my list of words I hate."

"—so he said it meant mental condition."

"What right does your dad have to say that?"

"He's a doctor."

I freaked. "He's a pediatrician! He can say that Oliver Voorhees shouldn't be driving because he's seven years old. But your father doesn't know *any-thing* about Sophie Gershowitz! Sophie Gershowitz, who incidentally is in top-notch mental condition, whose cognition is probably better than yours and mine put together, has been driving for a zillion years, maybe since before your father even went to medical school, and her only tickets have been parking tickets! Well, once she got stopped for sliding through a stop sign, but the cop just gave her a warning.

"So anyway, yes, we're going in her car to

Walmart to get her a new teakettle. Do you want to come? And what were you calling me about, anyway?"

"I wanted to tell you that my dad has a new updated Merck Manual and he said you can keep the one you borrowed."

That calmed me down a bit. Ralphie knows how much I love the Merck Manual. "Thanks," I said. "I've been using it a lot lately."

"What for? You got another fatal disease?"

(That was a somewhat unkind reference to the time recently when I thought I had pernicious anemia.)

"Ha ha. No, just ordinary stuff. You want to go with us, or not?"

"Okay, I'll go," he said. "What time are you leaving?"

We left at two thirty p.m. and got home at four forty-five. In between, Sophie Gershowitz bought a very handsome new teakettle, a whistling one (which I suggested, so that if she goes into another room, it will whistle at her and remind her that it is boiling), and I bought sunglasses that clip onto my plaid frames. Ralphie spent a lot of time looking at electronic stuff but ended up only buying a candy bar (I murmured *Junk food, Ralphie* but he pretended not to hear me), which was really just an impulse item at the cash register.

Sophie Gershowitz drove just fine, but unfortunately got lost on the way home. We found ourselves on the road to Manchester unexpectedly and had to get turned around. It was an error anybody might make.

CHAPTER

22

2. Short-Term Memory
Ask the patient to recall three objects after a
three-minute delay.

This was Question 2. Okay, full disclosure: I had done this with her already, right after the "What day is it?" question, and Sophie Gershowitz had flunked big-time. Twice, actually. My fault, really. I had not thought it through, just said three words and had expected it to be easy for her, but I was wrong.

I had said to her, "I'm going to name three things. And I want you to remember their names, and then when I ask you again after a little bit, tell me what they were."

"What are you talking about?" she said.

"It's a kind of test. Don't be embarrassed," I reminded her.

She waved her hand at me. It's a kind of thing she does, meaning: *You're bonkers.*

I ignored that.

"Okay, ready?" I said. "I'm going to say three words. Ready? Cat. Tablecloth. Chair."

Then I watched the clock. I hummed. I fiddled with the sugar bowl a bit. I threw a wadded-up piece of paper for Mr. Katz, who batted it around and then lost interest and walked away. Sophie Gershowitz went to the cupboard and got out a box of ginger-snaps, gave me one, and took one herself. When I had finished eating mine, the time was up and I said to her, "Now, please repeat the three words."

But she just looked at me with a puzzled look and said, "What three words?"

It was my fault, really. I think I botched giving her the directions. So I tried again.

I looked around the kitchen for some familiar objects. "Sophie, my dearest love," I said to her, "this is important. I'm again going to say three words and

I want you to remember them. Here they are: *Stove. Newspaper. Window.* Remember those."

I pointed to each thing as I said the word. Then I said them a second time, still pointing, I suppose just to press them into her memory, and mine. "*Stove. Newspaper. Window.*"

She shrugged. Then once again I had to kill three minutes. The Merck instructions didn't say what you were supposed to do during the three minutes. The instructions are very flawed, I think. This time I went and wiped off the top of the stove, which was kind of dirty from spilled soup. And I folded the newspaper. Then I breathed onto the window-pane and drew a smiley face in the steamed-up spot. Okay, I admit it: I was trying to reinforce the three words. *Stove. Newspaper. Window.*

Also, I should have set a timer. Too late. But when I glanced up at the clock on the wall, it seemed as if enough time had passed.

"Okay," I told Sophie Gershowitz. "Repeat those three words."

She looked blank. "What?"

"Remember I told you three words just a little

while ago? Tell me what they were."

"I can't," she said, after a moment.

Darn. It was really disheartening. I tried once more but got the same outcome. "I forget," she said. Three failures on Question 2.

We stared at each other. "It doesn't matter," I told her.

But it did. And now, after thinking about it for a bit, I had decided I would do that part of the test one more time. I thought I had figured out a new methodology. But for starters, I jumped over Question 2 and went to Question 3. Nowhere does it say that you have to do these questions in order.

Question 3 is easy. *Long-term memory* is its category. Ask the patient a question, it says, about the past, such as *What color suit did you wear at your wedding?*

"What color suit did you wear at your wedding?" I asked Sophie Gershowitz, and she gave me that squinty-eyed look that means she thinks I am bonkers.

"Suit?" she repeated. "Max Gershowitz, *he* wore

a suit at our wedding. Blue. Pants were too long. His mother should have shortened them. She was lazy. Max had a lazy mother. She never dried the dishes, just left them in a rack on the sink."

"Well, ah, what did *you* wear at your wedding?"

"You tell me, smarty-pants. What does a young girl, twenty years old, just learned English, never had a boyfriend before, what does she wear at her wedding?"

"This is supposed to be *your* test, not mine," I reminded her.

"Well, all right, I'll tell you then. I wore a black satin cocktail dress, skinny straps, boobies practically falling out if it. The rabbi nearly fainted when he saw me come down the aisle. I wiggled my hips. And I was smoking a cigarette, too."

She imitated smoking, sucking air between two of her fingers, jounced her breasts under her sweater, and hummed some suggestive music.

I started laughing. It was kind of shocking, actually. If anybody else—say, my history teacher, Mrs. Conant-Stewart—had suddenly started humming that way, and mentioning boobs, I would have been completely taken aback and maybe even called 911. But because it was Sophie Gershowitz, who had a way of making the most shocking subjects seem matter-of-fact, I started to laugh. "You're kidding," I said.

"You're right, my darling, I'm kidding, of course. So I wore a white dress with lace. It cost twenty-nine ninety-five, which was a lot of money in those days. And gloves—I wore white gloves. What else is new? Do I still get the prize?"

"You do, Sophie," I told her. "You get the prize."

CHAPTER

23

I was tempted to skip the math question, Question 4, because the book suggests asking the person (the book says "the patient" but I prefer to call her "the person") to subtract sevens, starting at one hundred. So the correct answer would be ninety-three, then eighty-six, then seventy-nine, etc. But that's *hard*. That's hard for *anybody*.

It suggests, alternatively, to ask the person how many nickels are in $1.35.

But who uses nickels? Nobody.

Sophie Gershowitz once told me that when she

came to the United States, age eighteen, she could get an ice cream cone for a nickel. She had never once had an ice cream cone in Poland, and she loved them so much that she spent all her spare nickels on them, sometimes didn't even have a regular lunch, just an ice cream cone with an extra scoop.

Today? To make a lunch out of ice cream would cost you a fortune. (Incidentally, Oliver Voorhees, brand-name expert and knower of all useless information, would be able to tell us the price of each of the different ice creams, and probably list the ingredients as well.)

In any case I think the question about nickels is an obsolete question. So I created an alternate one.

"There weren't any parking meters at the Walmart parking lot, were there?" I asked Sophie Gershowitz. "When we went to get the teakettle, you didn't have to put money in a meter, did you?"

"No, of course not. Parking's free there. Few things are free in this life, my darling. But Walmart's parking lot? It's one. You want more tea?"

I shook my head. She'd been making tea every

other minute since she got the new whistling tea-kettle. "What about when you go to that strip mall where you have your hair done?"

"What about it?"

"Are there parking meters there?"

She thought, then nodded. "Yes. I always try to get one that still has time left."

"Well, here's a question. Suppose you go there to get your hair done, and you park at a meter that has no time left on it."

"I got a parking ticket once. *Twenty dollars* because the meter expired. I think it was broken. I saw the woman writing the ticket and I went and told her the meter must be broken, but she didn't care, she ignored me. Wouldn't even look me in the eye."

"Yeah, that's too bad. But pay attention now because this is part of a test."

"And her penmanship was terrible." Sophie Gershowitz and I are both very upset about the lack of attention schools are paying to cursive.

"Anyway, suppose—"

"I suspect she dropped out of school. She'll never get a better job. Meter maid can't pay much. What if she has children to support? You need education."

"That's true. But listen, Sophie. Pretend you parked at a meter and there was no time on it, and the meter maid wasn't anywhere around, so we don't have to think about that. But pretend you're going to have your hair done, and it'll take an hour, maybe. So now you're going to put money in the meter, right?"

Sophie reached over to the coffee mug on the windowsill beside the kitchen table. It was filled with quarters. Every now and then she and I dumped the contents of her purse out onto the table, and we took all the quarters and put them in that mug. Other change went into a big beer mug left over from Aaron's college days. (It said *Colgate* on it. Why would you go to a college named for toothpaste?)

"So how many quarters are you going to need for the meter?" I asked her.

"You said for the beauty parlor?" she asked, and I nodded yes.

"A quarter buys fifteen minutes," she said.

"And you need an hour," I reminded her.

Carefully she counted out four quarters. She lined them up on the Formica tabletop.

"YES!" I said and gave her a fist bump.

"So I won the lottery again?"

"You did."

CHAPTER

24

Of course, I was planning to come back to Question 2, the one she had failed again and again, the one that most worried me. But after Sophie Gershowitz aced the math part by counting out the quarters for the parking meter, I went ahead to Question 5, *word finding*, which I knew would be super easy for her. It's just a matter of making lists in a category, and Sophie and I do that all the time.

"Now. A new part of the test," I told her. I didn't believe in concealing what I was doing. And anyway,

Merck says to tell the patient, and, you may remember, to assure the patient that it is routine and they shouldn't be embarrassed.

"It's routine," I said. "You shouldn't be embarrassed."

"I'm not embarrassed. You know who should be embarrassed? That cashier at Walmart. He had terrible body odor. He should use Right Guard."

She poured some more hot water over her tea bag. She really likes that new teakettle. "So. Ask me," she said, after she had swirled the teabag around a little and added a little milk and sugar.

"Okay, I'm going to tell you a category, and then you have one minute to list things in that category. Like if I said, oh, baseball teams, then you could list Detroit Tigers, Cleveland Indians—"

"Boston Red Sox," Sophie said. She and I follow the Red Sox religiously. (We talk often about Nomar Garciaparra. I never got to see him play because it was years ago, before I was born, but we both wish he still played for the Red Sox because it is a name that we love to say.)

"That's right."

"Baltimore Orioles."

"Yeah. That's enough, though, about baseball. It was only an example. I'm going to start the real test, now. Ready?"

Sophie Gershowitz sighed and rolled her eyes. I took that to mean *ready*. I looked at the second hand on her wall clock.

"Okay. Items of clothing. Go."

"Items of clothing?"

Oh, great. I should have just told her American League teams to begin with. She would have beaten the clock already.

"Yes. Things people wear. Like—oh, like *shirt*." I checked the clock again and waited till the second hand was at the top.

"Go," I said.

"Shirt," Sophie Gershowitz said.

"Good. Now keep listing them."

"List what?"

"Kinds of shirts!"

"T-shirt," she said. "Hawaiian shirt. Dress shirt. Nightshirt. Silk shirt. Long-sleeved shirt. Short-sleeved shirt."

"Good. Keep going." She had twenty seconds left.

"Ah, dirty shirt. Wrinkled shirt. See-through shirt."

"Okay. Time's up."

"Baseball shirt."

"You can stop now. Have a sip of your tea."

I decided to give her a perfect score on that part of the test because, let's face it, my instructions had not been good, and I thought her response was pretty imaginative even though it was not exactly what Merck had in mind.

At the back of my mind, floating there, I kept thinking about Question 2. The first time (*cat, tablecloth, chair*) she had flunked outright. I was too casual that first time. After I said the words, I had just fooled around, been silent, waiting for time to pass.

Then when I tried again (*stove, newspaper, window*), and threw in some clues, she had failed the second time.

Finally, the third try: *Teakettle. Jacket. Cup. Remember these words*, I had told her very firmly. Then, for the three minutes, I talked casually, but I talked about those things.

"I'm so glad we got that nice *teakettle*, aren't you?

"I think that new *teakettle* pours more easily than the old one. The water goes right into the *cup* without spilling.

"I always used to drip water from the old *teakettle* onto my *jacket*."

But when the minutes had passed and I asked her to repeat the three words, Sophie Gershowitz looked blank. "What three words?" she asked. "I forget."

I had thought of a new plan, now, for Question 2. I was still working out the details in my mind. But it seemed as if it might work.

CHAPTER

25

In the meantime: the sixth question. This tests, Merck says, attention and concentration. You're supposed to ask your patient to spell a five-letter word, first forward, then backwards. They suggest *world.*

I think that's actually pretty hard. When I tested myself (oh, did I forget to tell you that I tested myself? Well, of course I did), I had to stop and think about *world* for a moment, and picture the letters in my mind, before I could say "D, L, R, O, W."

But Merck didn't insist that you use *world.* I

reread the instructions, and Merck simply said "a five-letter word," and also "*world* is commonly used."

I decided against *world*.

"Sophie," I said to her, "I am going to tell you a five-letter word and I want you to spell it for me."

"Okay," Sophie Gershowitz said.

"First forward, then backwards."

"Why?"

"Because that's the test. You shouldn't be embarrassed."

"So who says I'm embarrassed? Give me the word, my darling. I'll spell."

"Nomar," I told her.

Sophie Gershowitz started to laugh. "N, O, M, A, R," she said.

"Now backwards."

"R, A, M, O, N."

"Correct."

"I win again?"

"You win again."

Sophie and I so loved Nomar Garciaparra. He made us laugh. He was her favorite baseball player *ever*: six-time All-Star, Rookie of the Year. But his name? That's why we laughed. He had been given his father's name—Ramon—spelled backwards. Who would do that to their baby? If Sophie Gershowitz had named her son Max, for his father, but backwards? He would be Xam.

If Ralphie Mariani had been named for his dad, Marco, backwards? Ocram.

The name Otto presents an interesting situation, but who in their right mind names a kid Otto?

(Or Nomar, for that matter. But I was glad that Mr. Garciaparra had done that.)

The seventh question of the test is so asinine. Give the patient an object—like a pen or a ruler—and tell him or her to name it. I figured I could get that one out of the way really quickly. I reached over, picked up the spoon that she had used to stir sugar into her tea, and handed it to Sophie Gershowitz.

"Name that," I told her.

She stared at the spoon for a moment. She turned it over and studied its underside. Then she said, "Mary Ellen."

Okay, okay. My fault. I had not given clear instructions.

I decided to redo Question 7. I went over to the stove and picked up the teakettle, which was on simmer, but it had a nice handle made of something that didn't get hot. "What's this? It's very pretty," I said to Sophie Gershowitz, as if I were seeing it for the first time.

"It's my new teakettle," she said proudly, clearly not remembering that I had picked it out for her at Walmart.

So? Who cares? She had named it. She passed the seventh question.

"Pass me the sugar, please," I said, and Sophie Gershowitz shoved the little blue-and-white bowl across the table to me. I spooned some sugar into my tea.

That was Question 8. *Following commands.* She aced it.

Question 8 had two parts, though. *Following three-part commands* was part two. "Sophie, my dearest love," I said (we like to call each other by extravagant descriptions), "Would you please go over to the radio and change the station to some better music?"

"So you're helpless all of a sudden?"

"No, but I don't know how to get the classical station."

"Ninety-nine point eight. Everybody knows that."

"I don't. Please, Sophie, would you go over and change the station and find ninety-nine point eight?" That made three verbs: go, change, find. A three-part command. "I am commanding you," I told her, but smiling so she knew I was joking. "I'm tired of the NPR news."

So Sophie heaved herself out of her chair (not easy—she needs new knees). "I'm not your servant, though," she said. "You fix lunch." Then she turned the dial to the classical music station, thereby fulfilling the requirement of Question 8.

She was on a roll. So I decided it was time to try again, using my new method, for Question 2.

CHAPTER

26

"I'm going to say three words," I told Sophie Gershowitz. "And I want you to repeat them—"

She interrupted me. "There's somebody at the door."

And sure enough, in a second, the doorbell rang. From where she was sitting, in the kitchen, she had seen someone come up the back steps to the porch.

It was Ralphie. He had Oliver beside him. Ralphie babysits for Oliver on days when Margaret Voorhees has to work late. It is a very, very easy job because Oliver Voorhees never misbehaves. He is absolutely attentive to good manners, to the point of being ridiculous. He becomes demanding only if his hair isn't combed properly (straight part, down the left side of his head) or if the silverware isn't lined up exactly right, and because he had been taught to shake hands in greeting someone, it makes him a little agitated if the other person doesn't hold out a hand. Stuff like that.

Incidentally, the hair-parting and handshaking are sort of connected. Let me explain. Oliver doesn't like to be touched. DOES NOT LIKE to be touched. Handshaking is, obviously, a kind of touching. His mom worked very hard with him to get him to understand that a handshake is a necessary thing, something he had to learn to endure. And so he does endure it, and more than that, he *requires* it because it is part of his politeness ritual. *But.* BIG but: he is so adorable to look at that sometimes a person who is introduced to Oliver—someone who doesn't yet know him well—will shake his hand and then reach out and tousle his hair. Or try to touch his cheek.

OMG. Big mistake. Meltdown time.

But all of us in the neighborhood know Oliver well, and we love him and we respect his limits. When I opened the door, there they stood, and Oliver immediately offered his hand and I shook it. But I glared at Ralphie.

"You're interrupting an important testing procedure," I informed him.

"Teddibly sorry," Ralphie said, and bowed. He does this sometimes, pretending to be upper-class British, kind of ridiculous if you are a short Italian kid, but he finds it amusing. "I accept your condemnation."

"Good day to you, Oliver," Sophie Gershowitz said, and reached over from her seat to give him a handshake. I kind of cringed because she had said "good day," which is not a perfect greeting for Oliver, because if it is raining, then he goes into a lengthy—and boring—explanation of precipitation and why it is not actually a good day. But today was. Blue sky, no clouds, light breeze.

"Can I make you some tea, Ralphie?" Sophie

Gershowitz asked him. "I have a wonderful new teakettle."

"I know. I was with you when you bought it at Walmart," Ralphie said. "Remember?"

"It whistles."

"Good. And thanks. But I don't like tea. Anyway, I just had a Pepsi."

"You just had a Pepsi? Talk about empty calories! Tell me that's not true." I looked daggers at Ralphie.

"Don't glare. I was thirsty."

"You didn't give any to Oliver, did you?" Oliver's diet was very carefully regulated.

"Of course not. Oliver had lemonade. Didn't you, Oliver?"

Oliver had been listening attentively. Now he nodded. "I had lemonade," he said, "with two ice cubes. Our Maytag refrigerator was purchased in 2017 and has an excellent ice-maker."

"And no Oreos, right? You didn't have Oreos, did you, Ralphie?"

"One."

I groaned. "Ralphie!"

"I know. I'm tapering off."

I just sighed. Later, maybe, I could give him one more lecture about the basic food groups, and how Oreos and Pepsi are not in them, but I know it's a lost cause.

"You can stay, Ralphie, if you want to, but you have to be quiet. I'm giving Sophie Gershowitz a test and we don't want any distraction. You can watch, but don't say anything."

"Okay." Ralphie settled back in a kitchen chair. Oliver went where he always does when he visits Sophie Gershowitz—into the hallway where Mr. Katz's bed was situated in a corner near the cellar door. He knelt there on the floor. Oliver is fascinated by Mr. Katz, though he is afraid to touch him. Oliver is very sensitive about the feel of things, and Mr. Katz's fur makes him nervous. But he loves watching Mr. Katz, the way his ears twitch, and how he sometimes flicks his tail a bit, even in his sleep.

"Would you like some tea, Ralphie?" Sophie Gershowitz asked.

"He already said no, Sophie. Now pay attention,

or we'll be here all afternoon."

She took a deep breath. "So," she said. "Test me."

"I'm going to say three words. Here's the first one: *Tree*. Repeat that."

"Tree." She repeated it, but with a suspicious look. "So, what am I, my darling, your puppet all of a sudden? What's that word, who's the man who doesn't move his mouth? Ventriloquist. Is that what you are, my darling? Are you wanting to hold me on your lap and make me say words to amuse an audience?"

"No, no," I told her. "Of course not. I'm sorry. But this is an experiment."

"Ha. So you're like Dr. Frankenstein."

I sent a daggery look at Ralphie so that he wouldn't be tempted to go into his Frankenstein imitation. "No," I said. "I'm not creating a monster. I'm actually testing a theory I have, about how to improve memory."

"You have a very scientific mind, for a girl. I'm glad of that. Girls should study science. Like my

Max did. Did I tell you that Max was a scientist?"

"Yes, you told me." I ignored that she had said "for a girl," which was sort of insulting, because I knew she didn't mean it that way. Actually, she had told me about her husband maybe a thousand times. He was a chemist. He retired when he was sixty-five years old. He went to bed that night, had a massive heart attack in his sleep, and never woke up. Maybe it was a world record: to retire from his job, retire to bed, and retire from life, all in the same twenty-four-hour period. Sophie Gershowitz has never stopped missing him.

"He graduated from Boston University. First person in his family to go to college."

"I know."

"He was a good man."

"I know he was."

"He always put the seat down. Three times a night he would get up. But he always—"

I interrupted her. "Whoa, wait. He what? Got up in the middle of the night? Why?"

"He had to you-know," she said.

Oh. I began to understand. He had to pee.

"It's a thing that happens to men," she explained. "Three times a night. And he always put the seat back down."

TMI. More than I wanted to know about Max Gershowitz. "Do you remember the word I told you to repeat a minute ago?"

She looked blank. "What word?" she asked.

I sighed. "*Tree,*" I told her. "We'll start over. Listen carefully. I want you to think of a tree."

This was my experiment, my idea—that if she could form a picture in her mind, maybe a picture with a little story attached to it, she would remember the word.

"A tree?" Sophie Gershowitz looked through the kitchen window, out into the yard, and to the woodsy area beyond, at all the trees there.

"Think back. When you were a little girl. Was there a particular tree that you remember?"

She closed her eyes. "*Jarzębina,*" she said.

"Excuse me?"

"Ah," she said, and opened her eyes and laughed a bit. "That was its name in the old country. Here we call it something different. I don't know what. People buy them. Isn't it funny how people buy trees? That big house up near the post office? You know the one I mean? They have this same tree in their yard. Probably it cost hundreds of dollars. Imagine that! In the old country no one would have spent money to buy a tree! Who could afford that? My darling, if I could take you there someday, show you that village! Trees grew everywhere. We had this tree in our garden. *Jarzębina.*

"Rowan tree!" she added suddenly. "That's what it's called here."

"Can you see it in your memory?" I asked her. "The one in your garden, when you were a little girl?"

Sophie Gershowitz nodded. "Oh yes, my darling. Filled with red berries."

"Good. Here's what I want you to do. Tell me a little story about that tree."

"A story?"

"Close your eyes. Think about the tree with the berries. Remember something that happened. You could even start with *Once upon a time.*

"Actually," I suggested, "they say that it is a good idea to start a story on a day that is different."

She sat silently for a minute. Ralphie and I did, too. We watched her. Her eyes were closed. She smiled a little. Then she began.

CHAPTER

27

*T*here was a—
    She paused, chuckled, and began again.

Once upon a time, there was a tree in our garden. I was a little girl. So the tree seemed very big to me, but probably it was not. Certainly not as tall as the fir trees in the forests that surrounded our village.

My sister, Chana, was a little older than me. Sometimes we would pick the red berries from the lowest branches, the ones we could reach, and we used them as playthings. We played counting games with them. And the game where you hide something in one hand, with your hands behind your back? We played that, with a fat red berry in one hand.

We didn't have toys bought from stores. We had dolls that our mother had made for us, with yarn for hair and buttons for eyes. How we loved those dolls! We would take them outside, into the garden, and serve them pretend tea, and little meals of bright red berries. We used leaves for dishes.

"Can you remember a particular day? A day that was different? Because sometimes a story should begin with—"

"Shhhh." Sophie Gershowitz held her finger to her lips, to shush me.

Summer had ended. The nights were chilly, but we still played in the garden after school, when the sun was shining. It wasn't winter yet. But the leaves on the trees were beginning to change color. And the berries on the jarzębina tree were plump and bright. The birds loved those berries. Sometimes our mother would try to shoo the birds away. "Leave some for us!" she would call out to them, and wave her apron.

"So you could eat them?"

Sophie nodded. "When they were ripe." Then she went on.

Every fall when the berries were ripe, we picked them. My big brothers used a ladder and picked the highest ones, and my sister and I gathered the ones that fell and picked from the low branches. Then our mother would make jam. She made enough to last through the winter. On the coldest days, with snow outside, we would have the jam on warm bread just out of the oven.

"What happened on the day that was different?" It worried me a little, that her story was veering off in other directions when all I really wanted was for her to think about a tree, picture a tree in her mind, remember a tree, and then, when I asked her, to say the word.

"Don't rush me, my darling. I'm getting there," Sophie Gershowitz said.

Our parents were not at home. My father worked long days at a factory. I forget what the factory made. Some sort of machinery parts. He came home after dark at the end of each day. And our mother—she worked, too. We were not wealthy people. She was the housekeeper for a rich family, the Gomolka family, who lived in a big house in town. And in the evenings, at home, she knit beautiful sweaters and shawls. People in town, those in the big houses, paid her for that.

My parents were not educated. But they saved and saved for the children to have a future. My big brothers—they were teenagers. One was to be a doctor, our parents said, and one a lawyer. They would go to the university. And—Oh yes! One of them was to play the violin! Whether he wanted to or not! Every night he practiced. The sound he made, it was terrible.

She laughed a little, remembering that.

"And the tree? What about the tree?" Okay, I was being a little impatient.

Shhhh. Just listen. When Chana and I came home from school, our big brothers looked after us. But we were good children. We did our schoolwork, and peeled the potatoes for supper, and when the sun began to set we lighted the lamps very carefully so that when our parents came home, everything would be warm and ready for the evening.

But on this day, the day that was different, it was still afternoon, and one of us—I think maybe it was Chana, she was always full of ideas—got the idea to pick all the berries so that they would be ready for the jam-making. The big boys got the ladder from the shed. And we brought baskets and filled them. We worked hard, laughing all the time as the berries fell into the baskets and on the ground, and finally the tree was bare. And we were so proud, because we had produced such a fine harvest and now everything was ready for our mamusia to fill the pots and add the sugar and start them simmering over the fire.

But then she came home, tired—she was always tired at the end of the day, because it was a long walk home after many hours of scrubbing floors and doing laundry. I remember she was carrying a bundle as she sometimes did. It might have been some of the family's outgrown clothing. Sometimes they gave her such things and she used the cloth or the unravelled yarn to make new things. Chana and I ran up the road to meet her. The big boys were out in the shed doing their chores, milking the goat, settling the chickens. She handed the little bundle to my sister, and took our hands, and we were so excited as we told her we had a surprise.

But as we came around the curve, she saw right away that the tree was bare. And we, my sister and I, saw right away that something was wrong because our mother's mouth made an O instead of a smile.

"We were very careful!" we told her. "The boys used the ladder, and we filled the baskets, and we didn't even step on very many. We picked up the ones that fell on the ground so they wouldn't get mashed!"

But she still wasn't smiling.

"What was wrong?" I asked Sophie Gershowitz. "Why was she mad?"

No, no, she wasn't angry. She hugged us both and told us she wasn't angry. She knew we had meant it as a wonderful surprise. She even said it was partly her fault because she had never explained. But the time was important. The time of picking the berries.

They could not be picked until after frost.

And there had been no frost yet. The ground was

still soft. The garden was still giving us some last vegetables. It was early fall, and the rowan berries would still be bitter. Too bitter for jam. If you picked the berries before frost, they would make you sick.

I got up from my chair and went to the stove and turned it on to heat water for tea refills. Ralphie had already said he didn't want any, and I didn't really care. But the room was so quiet when Sophie Gershowitz finished her story. It wasn't a sad story, not really. A winter without jam—that's not a tragedy. But there was a sadness to the way she told it. All the parts—the characters, the setting, the plot, all those things that you put together to create a story—there was something sort of *off* about them. Something that made me uncomfortable because I didn't understand it.

The teakettle began its cheerful whistle, and the atmosphere changed and became more lively.

"Well," I said, "you learned the hard way, didn't you?"

I brought her a fresh teabag and poured hot water over it.

"So you waited for the right time the next year, right? Waited till after frost?" I took the milk from the refrigerator.

She still didn't answer. It was as if she was still seeing the memory of it. And maybe that was a good thing, but I wondered why she looked so sad.

"What is the word that you're supposed to remember?" I asked Sophie Gershowitz.

She sighed. Then she said, "Tree."

CHAPTER

28

Ralphie took Oliver back to his house because it was time for *Judge Judy* reruns, which Oliver watched very attentively every afternoon. He could recite for you cases that dated back weeks, maybe months: all the details, how someone had not paid his rent because the landlord hadn't fixed a leaky toilet; or how someone's dog had growled at a neighbor's child from behind a fence and the child's mother thought the dog should be euthanized. It was really interesting to hear Oliver recount such court battles. Who would have guessed a seven-year-old could even pronounce *euthanize*? But he tended to go on a bit too long and it was hard to stop him once he got started.

Ralphie, as he was leaving, tried to pretend he was as excited as I was, that my strategy had worked. That remembering a tree, picturing a tree, had caused Sophie Gershowitz to overcome the blurry quality that was affecting her memory. Oh, sorry: her *cognition*. But let's face it: Ralphie has a limited attention span, and his interests are not always the same as mine. Plus, though he likes her just fine, Sophie Gershowitz is not his closest, dearest friend. So, after a few minutes of pretending he was thrilled at the way she repeated the word "tree," he looked at his watch and announced that *Judge Judy* would start in five minutes, and off he went, with Oliver beside him.

Me, I was on a roll. "Okay," I said, "you keep that tree in your mind. But now I want you to think of something else from your past. Think about the word *table*. Can you make a picture in your mind of a table?"

Sophie Gershowitz started to laugh. "Is this the

ugliest table you've ever seen?" she asked, tapping the surface beside her teacup on the Formica.

Well, it was, sort of. Speckled gray, chipped at one corner, with a rusted chrome strip around the edge. I didn't really want to agree with her because it's sort of rude to acknowledge the ugliness of other people's possessions.

But she didn't really need me to answer. "I should buy a new one. Do they sell tables at—what's that store we go to?"

"Walmart?"

"Walmart. I just bought something there, didn't I?"

"Yes, your teakettle."

"Shouldn't we go to Walmart again and buy something else? What was I just talking about?"

"Well," I told her, "you were talking about your table. I asked you to think of a table, the way you thought of a tree. Remember you thought about the tree from your childhood? And it made you remember the word 'tree.'"

"Tree," she repeated.

"Yes, and now I want you to think about a table. Maybe this one, or maybe some other table from when you were a little girl. Make a picture in your mind."

I got up and turned on the burner under the tea-kettle again. I was going to pour more hot water over her teabag. Or maybe she'd like a brand-new teabag? I reached into the box that held them and looked at her questioningly. Usually she would have said something like, "So, my darling, fill me up again, brand-new bag, let's live extravagantly, there's a good girl," but now she didn't even notice.

Her eyes had moved into a distant place. I waited, standing by the stove, for the water to boil.

29

*T*he legs were all carved, *she said suddenly.*
Flowers and leaves and some animals, too.
Yes. Krolicziki. Bunnies with long ears. I was very
small. Maybe four or five? And so that's what I saw
when I went to the bakery with my mother: the legs
of the table, because I was too little to see the top.

I caught the kettle before it began to whistle and
carefully poured hot water into her cup. I didn't
want to interrupt her. She was smiling now.

Yes, bunnies. My mother would be talking to the
baker and his wife, choosing what she would buy,

my sister standing politely at her side. *But I would lean in and touch the table legs with my fingers. I felt the carved ears and pretended the bunnies were real. There was flour on the floor around the table. Sometimes the baker's wife would be working the dough right there. What is you call that? Turning it, pounding with your hand—*

"Kneading," I said.

Kneading. Yes, she was kneading the dough. Little poofs of flour flew into the air and dusted my shoes.

"But the table?" I asked her. "Think about that. Was it a big table?"

Enormous. Right there in the center of the shop. Of course, it seemed huge because I was just a little girl then. But I know it was large, because of what happened.

"Something happened?"

Sophie Gershowitz began to laugh. *The baker and his wife had many children. Most families did, then. Our family was small, just four children, but I think there had been one or two babies after my big brothers and before my sister and me. My parents didn't speak of it. But I think perhaps there had been some losses.*

The baker's family, though—they seemed to have a new child every year! Little ones were always running about, in and out . . . I seem to remember twins hanging on to her skirt. She was Catholic, of course, like most of the villagers. They had big families. And I think she loved children. She always gave us something to nibble, maybe a broken cookie or even a little piece of apple, if she was making one of her apple pastries.

One day the bakery was closed. And when we went back the next day, what a surprise! There was a new baby! The baker's wife was sitting in a chair in the corner of the store and showed us the new little one, all swaddled tight, with a very pink face, sound asleep. She told us it was a boy.

And the baker was kneading the dough. Usually his wife did that. But he slapped it against the table and looked over and laughed. He said the baby had been born right there, on that very table! One day a loaf of bread, he said, and the next day a son! Who knows what happens tomorrow!

I remember my mother was a little shocked. As for me and my sister—what did we know about babies, how they came? Nothing at all. But Mamusia seemed shocked about the table. Later I would learn more. In those days the midwife came, and the babies were born in the family bed, where the mother and father slept. But at the time, when I was so young, it didn't seem shocking to me, only a little funny that the baker's baby son had arrived on the very table where they shaped the rolls and mixed the batters. Arrived how? Brought by a big bird? Those were the kind of stories children were told then. Chana and I whispered to each other that the baby might have raisins decorating his little belly.

Sophie Gershowitz took a sip of her tea. She was smiling at the memory of that time.

Then!" she added, suddenly. *This is now a long time later, you understand? That baby—by now he was a little boy, maybe two or three years old, and there was another, younger child. Probably also born on the same table! And one day the baker died, very suddenly. It was quite a shock to everyone.*

And you know what? They laid him out right

there, on that large table with the carved legs. There he lay, in his good suit, head at one end, feet at the other, on that very table where his babies had been born, where his wife had each day rolled dough and formed it into sweet rolls—drozdzówki z seremand. *Now people came and looked at the dead man's face and crossed themselves and prayed and paid their respects.*

"Did you see him there?" I asked her. "Was it weird? You were what, six by then? Seven?"

Oh, no. Things had changed. Things were different by then.

"What do you mean? Different how?"

We didn't go back to the bakery anymore. I guess we weren't welcome there. And we had stars sewn on our clothing. But I heard about the death of the baker. I heard my parents talk about it. And people said that his wife, after he was buried in the cemetery—there she was in the shop, again, rolling out the dough for the sweet rolls—on the same table.

"With the bunnies on the legs."

"With the bunnies." Sophie Gershowitz gave a hearty laugh.

I waited a moment and then I said to her, "Sophie, my dearest friend, what was the word I told you, the one I wanted you to remember?"

She was still chuckling a little and I could tell she was seeing, in her mind, the image of the baker, in his best suit, laid out on the . . .

"Table," she said. "Oh, my. That was it: *table.*"

I was thrilled. "Good for you!"

"So, I am passing another test?"

"With flying colors. And I have just one more for you."

"One more word?"

"Yes. Another word, another time for you to tell a story about the word. One more memory. Then you will have the three words, you will say them back to me, and the testing will be complete. Ready?"

She nodded.

I said, "Book."

CHAPTER

30

My mother couldn't read or write. Ah, I see the look on your face! But don't be shocked. It wasn't unusual then. Or in that place. Not in the small village where she had grown up and married and where we still lived. She had never been to school. But she was a smart woman, and a hardworking one. Up at sunrise. Doing the laundry, the ironing, the baking. Making breakfast for the family. Seeing everyone off: Papa to the factory, carrying his lunch. The children to school: clean clothes every day. School was everything. We were to read and to write. My brothers would be doctors, lawyers. They would play the violin, too. They had lessons each week from Mr. Raditsky; in return my mother did his mending, because his wife had died.

No music lessons for my sister Chana and me. But we would read. We would be educated women. A new generation! We would marry, of course, but we would not marry factory workers as she had. No. Though our father was a good man, an honest one, and he could read and took an interest in the world, he would always be poor. We, my sister and I, would not. We would be the wives of rabbis and judges. We would have servants, and nursemaids for our children. We would read books and attend concerts and have tea with our friends. Our parents' lives, their work, would make this all possible for us.

Each morning, after she cleaned up the kitchen, my mother removed her apron, attached a freshly ironed collar to her dress, wound her hair neatly into a roll that she pinned at the back of her head, and wrapped a knitted shawl around her shoulders. (This was winter, this time I am telling of. It was

cold there, in our village, often snowy.) She pulled
on her gloves and walked two miles to the fine home
of the Gomolka family. She was their housekeeper,
I've told you that already. She cleaned for them, and
did the laundry, and polished their silver. There was
a nursemaid for the little boy, Cyryl, but sometimes
my mother helped with his care as well. She made
sweetmeats for him and warmed his milk.

"Why did your mother have to work for someone else's family?"

Sophie Gershowitz shrugged. "I told you. We
were poor. They were rich. It was the way it was."

"But that wouldn't always be true," I pointed
out. "When your brothers got older and turned into
doctors and lawyers, then your mother wouldn't
have to work anymore."

"Exactly. So we thought. One day we would
have fine houses ourselves, and our mamusia would
sit in the parlor and maids would bring tea to her.
Our father would have a big comfortable chair and
would smoke a pipe, and our children would sit on
his knee and call him Dziadek."

"Why didn't that happen?"

There was a long silence. Then: "I am supposed to be telling you about a book, remember? Are you going to let me finish this story, or not?"

"I'm sorry. Go on."

One day my mother was dusting the library in the Gomolka house. There were walls of books. Janusz Gomolka was a professor. A great scholar. And he was a good man. He treasured those books, always touched them with respect, and so my mother did, too. She dusted them carefully and replaced them so that they were all lined up exactly.

And now for the day that was different. One day, because someone—perhaps the little boy, most likely the little boy—had pushed a book hastily onto the shelf, it was askew. Askew? Is that the right word?

"I think so. It means out of order. Crooked."

Yes. It was crooked in the shelf. So my mother removed it from its place, and saw that it was a child's book, a book of fairy tales. Baśnie braci. A corner of a page was bent, and she opened the book carefully and tried to straighten that bent place, to smooth it with her hand. And so she saw the illustrations. Paintings that showed the stories, and they were stories she recognized—"The Goose Girl," "Roszpunka" (you know that one, my darling? "Rapunzel"?), "Little Red Cap," and so many others—because she had heard them herself and retold them to us. "The Fisherman and His Wife!" It was there, she could see from the painting. And there were others, too, ones she had never heard.

She did something she had never dreamed she could do. No one was around. The child was napping. The wife was out for tea someplace. Father at the university. Nursemaid off an errand. My mother was alone. And she took the book of fairy tales to the small room off the kitchen, a sort of storage closet where she hung her shawl each morning. And she wrapped it in her shawl.

"Your mother stole the book?"

"No!" Sophie Gershowitz said. "She borrowed it! That was all! She wanted so much to show it to her own children! To me and my sister!"

"Okay. Okay. I get it. Relax. I don't blame her. People borrow books all the time. She probably should have asked, though. Go on. What happened?"

She thought she would keep it just one night.
Just to show her family. But there were so many sto-
ries in it! So many pictures! We begged and begged
her to keep it longer. And so she did. Each night,
after we had done our schoolwork, after our mother
had tidied the kitchen, Chana and I sat with her. My
sister was older. She could read better—

"How old?" I asked. "How old was Chana? And
you? How old were you?"

Silence again. Long silence. Then:

I think I was maybe eight. And Chana? She
would have been ten? She read the stories to us,
to Mamusia and me. "Rumpelstiltskin." "Clever
Hans." "The Juniper Tree." I remember them all
but I remember that one especially. Chana was in
the middle of reading that one on the night that our
papa did not come home. Mamusia was very wor-
ried. She kept going to the door and looking out
into the night. But he didn't come.

"What happened to him?" I asked. "Where was
he?"

She sent the boys out to inquire. It was snowing.
After a while they came back. They were clapping

their hands together for warmth. Snow made white fur over their hair. They told us what they had learned: that soldiers had come to the factory, the place where my papa worked, and took all the men away. People looking from windows, frightened, had seen them marching in rows, and there were soldiers with guns ordering them to walk faster, to stay in line. They were needed to work in another place, and they would go by train. A special train would come for them.

The next day, someone sent word, early in the morning, that my mother should not go to work. Her job was ended. She must not go to the Gomolkas' house again.

She sat for a moment, remembering, and I could not think of a question to ask her. Then she shrugged and spoke again.

After that, things happened very fast. I think it was all in a very few days. Hard to remember. Some of it is a blur. Soldiers came to our house. They looked for valuables but of course we had nothing. Just the candlesticks. They took those. And worst of all, they took the boys. My brothers: fifteen and seventeen years old. *Chana and I were hiding out-side, in the woods—Mamusia had told us to stay out of sight, and we hid in the fir trees but peeked out. When we saw the soldiers leave, with my broth-ers—they joined other boys out in the road with more soldiers and were marched away—we ran to the house and tried to comfort our mother. Things were broken and flung around. Our mother was weeping but she held us close to her, and when we asked, "What shall we do? What shall we do?" she shook her head as if she did not know.*

I wanted to ask, "Did you see them again, your brothers? Or your Papa?" but something made me stay silent. Something that knew the answer.

So, I was to talk about a book? Now we will go back to it, the beautiful book, because it was still there. The soldiers had left it. Dishes were broken but the book pages were not even torn. We read no more of it. We did not go back to school, for there was no school for us anymore—it was closed down and the windows broken. But the book was there, and each day as we tried to make sense of our life, tried to figure out what to do next, the book lay there unopened, because the time for stories was past. How would we eat, a woman and two little girls, and no work, no job anymore, no Papa, just potatoes and cabbages left from the garden, and still a few thin chickens out in the chicken house, but it was winter and the hens were not laying. The goat was gone. Who knows where?

Then one morning Mamusia told us to dress in our best clothes. She did, too. She warmed water at the stove and washed our faces. And she took the white lacy shawl that had been her mother's from the trunk where it was kept, and carefully she wrapped the book in it. She bundled us up and wrapped her own thick everyday shawl around her head and shoulders. She carried the package she had made with the book inside, and we walked with her through the snow, Chana holding my hand, down the narrow road that wound through our little village, and then farther, down the road that led to the larger town and to the Gomolkas' house. Our breath puffed out, little bursts of steam as we walked, into the winter air.

"Are you going to tell her that you took the

book?" I asked my mother when I realized where we were going. I was frightened. I had been punished harshly once, for taking something, a little carved toy that belonged to a friend.

"She is a good woman," Mamusia said. "A kind woman. I am going to explain that I borrowed it in order to show it to my children. She likes children. She has a little boy. Once she told me that she would like to have a daughter as well.

"I will apologize to her for borrowing it without asking permission. I will ask her forgiveness.

"And," she added, "I am going to ask for her help."

Listening to Sophie Gershowitz was like listening to a suspenseful story, something my teacher might have read aloud to us in school, stopping at the end of each chapter just when things were excruciatingly exciting. Even in fifth grade my teacher did that, especially for recess on bad-weather days when we had to stay indoors.

"What happened when you got to the Gomol-kas' house?" I asked when she had paused for so long that I couldn't stand it.

There was a door knocker, I remember, brightly polished. I thought it was gold. Now I realize it was probably brass. Shiny, shiny. My mother told Chana and me to wait below, at the foot of the stairs that led to the door. We stood there. Our feet were very cold and we stamped them up and down a bit to warm them. We watched as our mother went up the steps and lifted the shiny door knocker and let it thump against the door. We saw someone draw a curtain aside and look out at us through a window. After a moment my mother knocked again and finally the door swung open.

It was Mrs. Gomolka herself who came to the door. Beside her a little boy with blond curls was holding her skirt. When the little boy saw my mother he laughed and held his arms up, but Mamusia did not look at him, and his face become puzzled. She talked to the woman and we could not hear the words. She was speaking in a low voice, the kind of voice you use to make an apology. Przepraszam. I am sorry. We saw her hold up the wrapped package of the book and place it in the woman's hands. We saw the woman nod. She was listening to Mamusia.

She was not smiling but she had a kind look on her face, and when she tried to unwind the lacy wrapping, my mother shook her head, held up her hand, and we knew she was telling the woman that the white shawl was a gift.

The woman nodded, and murmured some words, and then she tried to close the door. But Mamusia stopped her. She began talking very quickly in a desperate voice, and we could see her turn and point to us below. The woman kept responding in a kind voice—a sympathetic voice—but she also kept turning away as if to close the door.

We heard our mother crying. We heard her beg.

Finally, the woman drew a deep sighing breath and she stepped forward a bit from the open door and looked down at Chana and me.

Then at last she nodded her head, and our mother bent down to kiss her hands. But the woman lifted one hand and held it up with one finger extended. Tylko jeden, she said. Just one. She pointed to me.

And Mamusia knew she could not beg for more. She turned and called gently to me to come.

I let go of my sister's hand and climbed the steps

alone. And that is how a book paved the way for me to become, for a time, Zofia Gomolka. I became the daughter of a Catholic family in a small city in Poland. And so, my darling, I was saved.

We sat in silence for a moment. Then, after a moment, I said, stupidly, "Sophie, my dearest one, tell me the three words that you were supposed to remember."

She looked away. "It was wartime," she said.

"I know. World War Two."

"You study it in school?"

I nodded. "Yes," I said, "and I get As in history always. I memorize the dates and the names of the battles, but . . ."

I didn't complete the sentence and finally, in the silence, she asked, "But what, my darling?"

"Those things aren't enough," I whispered. "You can't feel them. You need the stories."

Sophie Gershowitz was silent for a moment. Then she reached toward me, took my hand, and held it. "My darling girl," she said, "I have never told anyone these stories. For all these many years my mouth has not been able to make the words.

Not even to Max. Or Aaron."

I didn't reply. I didn't know what to say.

"Only now, suddenly, to you, I needed to tell them."

We sat silently, and she stroked my hand.

Then she said, abruptly, "I don't remember the three words."

"*Tree*," I told her. "*Table. Book.*"

She sighed. "Yes. And you have them now, with their stories. Keep them close. Hold on to them tightly for me. Don't forget them."

CHAPTER

31

During the time that Sophie Gershowitz told me the story of the book, the sun had moved across the roof of her house and was sinking lower in the sky behind her backyard and garage. Rain clouds appeared. It was actually becoming chilly. I could have redone "following three-part commands" question, Question 8, and said, "Sophie, my dear one, turn the kitchen light on, and then hand me my sweater, and get a Lean Cuisine dinner out of the freezer." She would have done those things, I am quite sure. But I didn't feel like testing her anymore.

Instead, I reached over to the light switch and flicked it so that the ceiling light came on and everything looked suddenly harsh and flat and overly bright. Mr. Katz appeared from the shadows of the hallway where he had been sleeping in his fleece-lined bed. He glanced at his empty bowl on the floor under the window and meowed loudly as if he'd been insulted.

Halfheartedly, since it didn't seem to matter anymore, I asked Sophie the "abstract reasoning" question. *Ask the patient to identify a unifying theme between three or four objects (e.g., all are fruit, all are vehicles of transportation, all are musical instruments).*

She had heaved herself up out of her chair and was getting the Meow Mix from the pantry.

"Cat, dog, hamster, gerbil," I said loudly to her. "What do those things have in common?" I figured I could accept "animals" or "pets," either one.

She turned and looked down at the dish, at the cat, at the bag of Meow Mix in her hand. She looked confused.

"They all had mothers?" she asked.

CHAPTER

32

Way back, many pages ago, when I began to tell you this story about Sophie Gershowitz and me, I listed three words for you and told you to remember them.

They were pretty simple words. Nothing complicated.

Tell me what they were.

You can't, can you? See? SEE?

CHAPTER

33

On Friday afternoon I was at home, depressed, watching my mother put together dinner for company. She said she didn't need any help, but I hung around the kitchen anyway, watching as she combined noodles and chicken and sour cream and mushroom soup in a heavy red casserole, and sprinkled bread crumbs over the top. Through the window I could see that the house across the street, the fixer-upper, had made a geometric shadow across its front yard in the late-afternoon light.

"Even though that house is pretty shabby," I said

to my mother, "don't you think there's a comfortable quality about it? Like, *cozy?*"

She laughed. "If you like the smell of mold."

Dutifully I chuckled. "No, I meant that if you wanted to be alone, maybe, and in a really private place—maybe if you were very old, for example—it would be nice and quiet there."

"Wrap that loaf of garlic bread in aluminum foil, would you, please?"

It was probably a good thing that she wasn't paying any attention to what I was saying, because I knew it made no sense. But I thought of Catsy, enjoying the solitude, watching the night come, wherever she had gone. And purring, maybe. And I thought of Sophie Gershowitz, and—well, of course it wasn't the same thing, not at all, but still: Doesn't everyone deserve to have a special place?

The little red light on the stove said that the oven was heating. The company would be Aaron Gershon, who was due to arrive shortly, and his mother. She would hold on to his arm as he brought her across the yard to our door, and even though she had said quite clearly again and again to me that Aaron from

Akron was an Annoyance, I knew she would look pleased and proud to have her arm in his, and his hand cupped over her hand.

Ring ring. Phone. I told my mom I'd get it.

"Hello, Winslow Real Estate."

"*Ciao.*" (Italian greeting, in case you don't know already.)

"Hi, Ralphie."

"How did she do?"

"What do you mean?"

"You know, the test. I left after she told the story about the tree and the berries."

"Oh. Okay, I guess." (That phrase—*okay, I guess*—is a complete cop-out phrase. You can use it to answer almost anything and it will conceal your real feelings without being a lie.) I could tell that he wasn't that interested anyway.

And for some reason I didn't want to tell Ralphie the truth. I didn't want to tell him the story about the table, even though it was sort of funny. I certainly didn't want to tell him the story about the book, because it was the saddest and most private story I had ever heard. And especially I didn't want to tell him that the stories didn't work, that they didn't cause Sophie Gershowitz to hold on to the three words, and in fact the stories had plunged me into despair because now I knew her history and her future, both at the same time, and both of them made me feel hopelessly sad.

"Guess what? I found a way to get into the haunted house."

That was the fixer-upper, the same house that had been in my thoughts for the past few days.

"Yeah." I waited.

Silence. Then: "Aren't you interested?"

"Oh, I thought that was number one. I was waiting for number two. I thought it was two truths and a lie."

"No, I'm not playing a *game*, Sophie. I really did find a way to go in. After *Judge Judy*, I took Oliver out for another walk and we went around to the back of the haunted house. And the kitchen window that opens onto the back porch? The screen is all broken. I just lifted it off and the window was unlocked. So Oliver stayed on the porch because he was lining up the flowerpots, and I climbed in and looked around, and then I came back out through the door, and I left the door unlocked so we can go in and explore."

I didn't say this to Ralphie, but the truth is, *of course* I was interested. It was why I had just mentioned it to my mom. It was why I found myself staring at it, or at least at the thick trees that concealed the front of it, all the time. From where I was standing with the phone, I glanced through our living room window and once again I could see it there. The For Sale sign was only partly visible because an overgrown hydrangea had spread across the E. The fixer-upper was now For Sal.

No, it wasn't! It was For Sophie Gershowitz. I had a passionate feeling that I could make that come true.

I could also see into the kitchen. I watched my mother lift the heavy red cast-iron casserole into the oven. Then she got a bunch of salad things out of the fridge and started washing lettuce. She was humming.

My dad would come from the office soon. Then Aaron Gershon would drive up next door and lift a suitcase out of the trunk of a rental car, and after a bit he'd hold out his arm to his mother as if he were her date for the prom, and they would come across the lawn for dinner. Then we would all sit around eating chicken casserole and noticing how Sophie Gershowitz looked confused most of the time and kept watching other people to see how, exactly, to use a fork, but we would be cheerful and smile and pretend everything was okay, and so would she. And it would be okay for Aaron, and for my parents, because they had a *plan in place*, but it was not okay for me because my heart was breaking.

The next morning, he would take her to the doctor, who had agreed to a special Saturday meeting just for this purpose. Sophie Gershowitz would have her stupid *cognition* tested, and she would fail, and then he would start packing her things and throwing stuff away (my mother always called it "downsizing" and "decluttering" to clients on the phone, using a cheerful voice) and he would take her to live in a place where no one would know who she was or what her life had been like or who the heck Nomar Garciaparra was. He would do that *unless*. Unless I could change things.

I half listened to Ralphie yammer on, *blah blah blah*, and I began to think again about my very small, completely weird idea, which made no sense, and was also dangerous and illegal. But having an idea makes you feel less helpless.

"I have to go, Ralphie. I promised my mother I'd help with dinner."

"Wait. One more thing. The big house up by the post office, with the tree that has the red berries? I asked my mother about it and she said it's a mountain ash. So that other name, the one Mrs. Gershowitch said, was wrong."

For some reason it made me very angry, that Ralphie not only mispronounced my best friend's name but was also nitpicking about something that didn't matter.

"I'm going now, Ralphie."

"Oh. Okay. *Arrivaderci.*"

Grudgingly I muttered *Sayonara* and hung up the phone.

CHAPTER

34

Usually on Saturdays Oliver goes with his mother on some kind of excursion. Once she took him all the way to Boston to the Museum of Science. Oliver was still talking about that, especially about the Hall of Human Life, which was his favorite part.

"At the Hands-On Laboratory, you can use the same tools and techniques as real scientists," he explained to me several times.

"Great," I told him. "That's very cool."

"I am not a real scientist, but I used the same

tools and techniques as a real scientist."

"Maybe someday you will be a real scientist," I said.

Oliver thought about that. "No," he said. "I want to be an architect."

Oliver, wearing his favorite *Star Trek* T-shirt, was with Ralphie and me even though it was Saturday, because this morning his mother had a job interview. At the newspaper! They were looking for someone to write classified ads. Margaret Voorhees felt certain that would be a job with more upward mobility than restaurant hostess. She might go on to be a reporter, she thinks, or an editor. She'd been practicing for the interview by thinking of ways to improve the ads that were in the paper. For example: *Free kittens to good home* probably didn't attract a single taker. But what if it said: *Adorable kitty cats with big soulful eyes and the sweetest purr. No charge!* Well, maybe.

So we had Oliver with us for the morning. My dad was off at open houses—those were always held on weekends—and my mother was "womanning" the phones in the office. Ha ha. That's what she called it, instead of "manning."

We were on our way over to the fixer-upper. Dinner last night had been okay, even though Aaron Gershon was pretty boring, talking about changes in the tax laws and stuff like that. But he had been super attentive to his mother, and she seemed really glad to have him there. He asked her if she wanted second helpings, and he kept including her in the conversation, saying things like, "Isn't that right, Mother?" and leaning down to pick up her napkin when it slid off her lap. Now and then she reached over and patted his hand where it rested on the table. I could tell that she was remembering when he was an Eagle Scout, or maybe the time when he made her a valentine in first grade, and it said *Bee Mine* and had a picture of a bumblebee. I know about this because she kept it all those years, in a box with his report cards: all As, all As, all As. Once a B in European history, but she said he had a bad teacher that year.

Aaron didn't seem such an Annoyance at dinner, not when he was being so attentive to his mother. But I kept thinking, *He doesn't know. He doesn't know about her tree, or her table, the things she had told me. He doesn't know about the book, how it was carefully wrapped in a white shawl. Someone who knows about changes in the tax laws does not understand the human heart and how it can break. If he did, he would not take Sophie Gershowitz away from me.*

And because I knew his evil intentions, I mentally cursed him with the Chocorua Curse while we ate. Silently I asked the Great Spirit to make wind and fire destroy his home, though not when his mother was in it, and to breathe death on his cattle. And also, during dessert, I added (silently) *P.S. May wolves fatten on your bones.*

The three of us ducked through the overhanging bushes in front of the fixer-upper, went through the yard, which needed mowing again, and around to the back porch. Oliver had brought one of his favorite tools . . . a yardstick with *Ace Hardware* printed on it. He used it as a walking stick as we made our way through the overgrown shrubbery and up the splintery steps.

"This house *really* needs TLC," I commented. I could see where the window screen was torn, and how Ralphie had gotten inside.

Oliver looked up. He was on his knees now and had placed his yardstick carefully on the floor of the porch. He was going to measure. Oliver loved measuring things. "TCM is the movie channel," he announced. "It means Turner Classic Movies."

"Yeah," I agreed.

"OWN is the Oprah Winfrey Network," Oliver said.

"I know that."

"Why does this house need the Learning Channel?" he asked.

I laughed. "I didn't mean a TV channel," I told Oliver. "I was talking about special initials, and they mean 'tender loving care.'"

He nodded.

"Tender loving care," he repeated to himself, thinking it over while he nudged the end of the yardstick up against the wall that bordered the porch. "Tender loving care.

"Three feet," Oliver announced, and lifted the

yardstick carefully to add the next measurement.

"Hey, Oliver," Ralphie asked him, "why can't someone's nose ever be twelve inches long?"

Oliver looked up, puzzled, and felt his own nose.

"That's mean, Ralphie. Don't do that," I said.

But Ralphie ignored me. "Because then it would be a foot!" he announced, chortling.

Oliver still looked puzzled. "I think my nose is about an inch," he said. "Nobody's nose would be—"

"It's a joke, Oliver. Because it would be a foot, not a nose. Get it?"

But he didn't. "A foot is twelve inches," he said. "Nobody's—"

"It was just a stupid joke, Oliver," I explained.

Oliver still looked confused, but Ralphie had lost interest and was examining the back door. "Here I go!" he announced. He pulled open the battered screen door, entered through the unlocked wooden door, and disappeared into the house.

Oliver began to arrange his yardstick carefully on the porch floor. I watched him for a few moments, then said, "I'm going to find Ralphie. I'll be back in a minute. You keep measuring the porch, okay?"

He nodded and leaned over to examine the numbers on his yardstick.

Ralphie appeared suddenly in the window with the torn screen and said, in his game-show-host voice, "Enter and sign in, please."

I went into the house through the back door.

CHAPTER

35

Houses that haven't been lived in for a while have a musty, empty quality. This one did, at least. It was dim inside (though the lights worked—I tried one, the electricity was on) because there were no picture windows, the kind of thing a ranch-style house would have. This house had just regular old windows and hanging over them were faded curtains that filtered the daylight. There was dust on the tabletops, and the upholstery on the living room couch was faded and worn. You could almost tell where people had sat in the past, because the cushions sagged in places. Ugly shag carpeting in need of cleaning covered the floor, and you could see the lines where a vacuum had been swooshed through (probably by the real estate agent, guess who).

The TV was an old one and there was a remote on top of it, but I didn't turn it on.

"Just this one old remote. That's good."

"Why is that good?" Ralphie asked. He picked up the clicker and examined it. "This is really out of date. You can't record with it or anything. And there's no *guide*."

"Because if an old person lived here, that person would just have to click on and off and wouldn't have to fool around with a lot of stuff. Old people don't understand smart TVs. They get volume and channels and that's about it, but it's all they need."

"Look, the phone's really old fashioned, too," Ralphie said. He lifted the receiver from a black tabletop phone and listened briefly. "It's not connected. Totally dead.

"*Moshi moshi*," he said to the silent telephone, and replaced its receiver. (Japanese. I told you that already.)

"Let's look in the kitchen," he said, "and see if they left anything in the refrigerator." He headed into the hall that led to the kitchen. "I bet they don't even have an ice-maker," he added.

The kitchen actually reminded me a little of Sophie Gershowitz's kitchen, the place where I spend so much time. There was a similar Formica table, with rusted metal on its edges. Someone had left a coffee mug on it, with some sludgy looking brown stuff in its bottom. We opened a few cupboards— all empty—and drawers lined with stained paper. The drawers had crumbs in their corners, and were strewn with something else, like maybe peppercorns. "Mouse poop," Ralphie announced.

I shuddered. Then I thought for a moment and said, "A cat would take care of any mice."

"Then you'd have *cat* poop."

"No, you wouldn't. Cats are very clean. He uses a litter box."

"What do you mean, *he?*" Ralphie opened the refrigerator.

I ignored his question. But of course, I had been thinking of Mr. Katz.

"Hey, look!" He leaned into the open refrigerator and picked up a little orange box. "They left something."

"It's baking soda, Ralphie. People keep it in the refrigerator to absorb odors."

Ralphie sniffed. "Well, it quit working. Look, there's a place where something spilled and it ran down the side and froze there." He pointed to a bright-colored streak of solidified something stuck to the inside wall of the refrigerator. "Orange juice, I bet."

I ignored him, as I sometimes do (it doesn't matter if you ignore Ralphie; he just keeps talking), because I was looking around, imagining how a person would live in this somewhat shabby, slightly old-fashioned house. At first I pictured it like a dollhouse (my own is up in the attic now, but when I was younger I played with it for hours), as if I were leaning in and rearranging the furniture a bit, and then moving the little dolls with their bendable legs and arms, seating one on the couch with the faded upholstery, maybe standing one in front of the sink, reaching her tiny plastic hands in to wash a miniature bowl.

Then I realized I was envisioning Sophie Gershowitz, sitting in one of the chairs of the matched set—*dinette set*: that's what she called hers—that was arranged around the Formica table. On the stove, on a back burner, was her whistling teakettle from Walmart, and Mr. Katz was in his comfy bed in the corner.

It was the fantasy I'd been having now for several days, and I knew it was crazy, I knew it couldn't happen, I knew all that, I really did, and yet I found myself seeing her there in my imagination, and I was thinking: *yes, we could do this, we could make this happen, and no one would* . . .

"Earth to Sophie?" Ralphie was standing in front of me, waving his hand as if he were trying to wake me up. And it was true; I was just semi-alert; most of my brain was in a dreamlike place and I had vaguely heard him talking about the ice-cube trays he'd found in the freezer, but . . .

"Ralphie," I said, in a low, secretive voice, "forget

ice-makers. Listen: We could smuggle Sophie Gershowitz in here. Bring her clothes and her cat and everything. We'd do it after dark. No one would even know she was here."

"*What?*"

"We could save her, Ralphie! Her son wants to put her in some kind of old-people institution. It's not fair. He's going to force her. He's going to make her get into that car, and he'll take her to Boston to get on a plane and—"

"That's kidnapping," Ralphie pointed out. "We should call the police."

"Well, if he actually did it, and it was against her will, then we could call the police, I suppose. But it would be better if we *prevented* it, Ralphie. And we could do that by bringing her over here and hiding her here in the fixer-upper."

"That would *definitely* be kidnapping," Ralphie said.

"No, it wouldn't. She'd come willingly. It would be an adventure. We'd bring Mr. Katz, and all the stuff she likes, her magazines and newspapers, her new teakettle, her knitting basket, so it would be familiar. And we'd visit her all the time. She—"

Ralphie was looking at me as if I had lost my mind, and maybe I had.

Yes, I guess I had.

But then, before we had a chance to think it through, there was Oliver, who appeared in the kitchen holding his yardstick and making an announcement.

"Ten feet and three inches across," he said. "And fourteen feet and two inches long. If it were ten feet and three inches long, it would be a square. But instead, it's a rectangle."

"*What's* a rectangle?" I asked him.

"A figure with straight but unequal sides," he explained.

Wouldn't you expect a seven-year-old to say, *It's a thing like a square but it's longer on two sides*, and hold up his hands to draw a picture of it in the air? But not Oliver Voorhees. He thinks, and talks, like an adult. I admire that.

"No, no, I meant what rectangle are you describing?"

"The back porch."

"Oh." Back porch; back porch. Of course, Oliver had been out there with his yardstick. I was still trying to shake myself loose from the fantasy about Sophie Gershowitz.

"Hey. Oliver! What do you call an angle that gets into an accident?" Ralphie asked.

"Ralphie, *don't*," I said. "Oliver doesn't . . ."

But Ralphie paid no attention. "A rectangle! Get it? A wrecked angle?"

"Yes, I get it," I said. "Ha ha."

But of course, Oliver didn't. "You mean a car accident? How can an angle be in an accident?"

I began to try to explain but once again Ralphie interrupted me.

"Look at these," Ralphie said in a disgusted voice. He was holding up a metal ice tray. "These are so gross. When were ice makers invented? This fridge is *ancient*!"

"The 1950s," Oliver announced. "But they were very primitive at first. Then in 1965 Frigidaire made one that was built into the—"

"Oliver," I asked, "are you sure you're only seven? Maybe you're really *seventy*?"

He appeared to be considering that. Then he said, "Yes. I'm seven. I was born on October twenty-first, in two thousand—"

I interrupted him. "Of course you are. I was just sort of jok—well, not really joking, but commenting on the fact that you know as much as a guy who's way older than you. It's really quite amazing, Oliver. Is there *anything* that you don't know?"

He nodded, with a solemn look. "Yes," he said. "Many things." He frowned.

I could tell he was going to start listing things. I love Oliver Voorhees, but when he begins listing things, it's almost impossible to make him stop. So I interrupted him again.

"Come on," I said. "Let's go home. Ralphie, put the ice trays away. And be sure to lock the back door this time. We shouldn't have been in here."

"So you're not still thinking about—?"

"It was a dumb idea."

"Yeah, it was. But hey: We could make it work. Maybe we could tell her it was just temporary, like while her house was being painted or something, and then she—"

Oliver looked up. "Who?" he asked. We were on the porch by now, and Ralphie had turned to close and lock the back door. "Whose house was being painted?"

"Nobody. We were just talking about—"

I was going to make up something. But Ralphie caught up with us and said, "Mrs. What's-her-name. Over there, with the cat." He pointed across the street.

"Sophie Gershowitz," Oliver said. He never forgets a name. Or a statistic, or a little-known fact, for that matter. "Are they painting her house? Are they using Benjamin Moore, or Sherwin-Williams?" he asked. He had a thing about brands, even brands of paint. "Or they could use Farrow and Ball, but it's way expensive. It's luxury paint.

"Movie stars use luxury paint. I think Judge Judy probably uses it."

"I'm sure she does," I told him. I was glad he'd changed the subject. I almost put my arm around him until luckily I remembered that Oliver doesn't like being touched.

But leave it to blabbermouth Ralphie. "We were

thinking about hiding Mrs. Gershowitch in this house. Nobody would know she was here. Nobody but us, of course, and we wouldn't tell."

"Why would you hide her?" Oliver asked.

"Because if we don't, we might never see her again. She might move away."

"Why?"

I interrupted them. "It was just a stupid idea, Oliver. It was a sort of a game we were playing, pretending we could hide her."

"Would she be all alone in the fixer-upper? It wouldn't be familiar. She'd be very scared."

"We'd visit her," Ralphie said with a shrug. I was getting kind of mad at Ralphie. It had been my idea in the first place, even if it was a dumb one, but now he was grabbing it away from me, and making it sound like a real plan.

"Look! There she is! Let's go and ask her if she wants to move to the fixer-upper!" Oliver pointed through the shrubbery, and across the street, and sure enough, there was Sophie Gershowitz in her driveway. Her son was helping her into the front seat of his car. I looked at my watch and realized they were headed to her doctor's appointment.

"No, no," I told Oliver hastily. "It was a secret plan. Don't tell. Anyway, it's not going to happen."

"I know why it isn't going to happen," Oliver commented as we watched the car drive away. I waved but Sophie Gershowitz didn't see me. She was turned toward Aaron. They were laughing.

"Do you? Why is that?"

Oliver tucked his yardstick carefully under his arm. Then he looked at the ground and began twisting his fingers together, as he always did when he was thinking. After a moment he looked back up and said, "You could not hide Sophie Gershowitz in the fixer-upper because it would not be TLC."

He nodded in agreement with himself and repeated it. "Not one bit TLC."

Have I explained to you that true friends learn from one another? Have I mentioned that Oliver is filled with wisdom, and that he will always be a true friend?

CHAPTER

36

Margaret Voorhees didn't get the job. She came
home from the interview disappointed but
trying to be cheerful and good-sport-ish.

She didn't have any experience, they had said.

Ha. She had seven years of experience being
a great mom to a very unusual boy. She had eons
of experience at the Chocorua Bar and Grill. She
had experience being nice to demanding customers
who arrived right at the busiest time and said that
they had made a reservation when they *hadn't*, or
who ordered the special but wanted it without the

broccoli and could they have extra mushrooms on their steak and also no cucumber in their salad, or who were seated long enough to unfold their napkins and mess around with the silverware and then called her over and said they wanted to change tables and be over there closer to the window. All of that. She did it day after day, and she also was pleasant and polite to men customers who looked at her nametag and called her Maggie or Meg or Peggy instead of her name, Margaret, and asked what time she got off and would she like to go out for a drink after work, and then when she pleasantly and politely said *no thank you*, they turned surly and rude and made hateful remarks—one even said who did she think she was, Princess Margaret?—on their way out.

But the newspaper person said they were looking for someone with experience.

I told my parents I wanted to stick pins into a voodoo doll that looked like the editor in chief, but my dad said that wouldn't be productive or helpful.

"What *would* be productive and helpful?" I grumbled.

"Your mom and I are going to ask Margaret if

she'd start writing the ads for our inventory."

"You mean the houses for sale?"

"Yes. And for open houses. She could do it in her time off from restaurant work, and it would provide her with some experience. Maybe in another few months, or next year, the newspaper would be willing to give her a job."

"You think? And then she could work her way up to reporter, or editor, and eventually she could maybe run the whole paper? And by then Oliver will be old enough so that she could give him a job? Because let's face it, Dad: Oliver is very, very smart but he's probably always going to have a hard time, and—"

He started laughing. "Whoa," he said. "Slow down."

"Okay. But still."

"It will be a start for her, Soph. And we'll all hope for the best. That's all we can do. Start small."

I'm not convinced that it is all we can do. But for now, I'll take my dad's advice and hope for the best. Especially when it comes to Sophie Gershowitz, who of course hadn't done very well on her cognition test, at least not by the stupid standards of the neurologist that her son Aaron took her to.

"My darling, my darling," she said to me, when I went over to see her on Sunday morning, "where have you been?" I hadn't seen her since Friday night's dinner at my house, except when she sat in the car laughing beside Aaron as they drove off on Saturday.

"You were busy with Aaron yesterday," I pointed out, "and I helped Ralphie babysit Oliver."

"You're a good, helpful girl," she said, and patted the knee of my jeans when I sat down beside her at the dinette set.

"You know what day it is?" I asked her.

"Is this another test and I shouldn't be embarrassed?"

I laughed a little. "No. We're done with the tests. I'm just reminding you that it's Sunday. Church day."

"I know, I know. Those bells! They think it's a competition, like the Olympics."

Our little town has a zillion churches, and they all ring their bells on Sunday morning. I had seen the Mariani family get into their station wagon and head off to mass. And Margaret Voorhees had buckled

Oliver, wearing his little bow tie—he loves his bow tie, but she won't let him wear it to school because she fears his being laughed at—into the back seat and they had left for the Methodist Church, where Oliver attends Sunday School.

My family doesn't go to church. My parents have to deal with open houses almost every weekend, and on Sunday mornings my mother usually loads our vacuum cleaner into the car and goes off to smooth out yesterday's footprints from the carpeting and to rearrange the little brochures that are stacked neatly inside every house for sale.

But Sophie Gershowitz and I have our own personal Sunday morning ritual. That's why I had reminded her of the day.

We arranged ourselves and sat quietly for a moment with our hands folded. Then:

"Kindness," I said to Sophie Gershowitz.

"Kindness," she said in reply.

We always have a moment of silence after we say *Kindness*, and we are supposed to be thinking thoughts about kindness during that moment.

Sometimes, though, like today, I have a hard

time with that part. "Where's the Accountant from Akron this morning?" I asked her, after our silent moment.

I wanted her to say, "You mean the Annoyance? He's gone back home."

But instead, she smiled. I realized that unlike me, she actually had been thinking *Kindness*. "Such a good son. He made me scrambled eggs," she said. "And now"—she nodded her head toward the hall and the staircase, and when she did that, I could hear Aaron's voice from another room, murmuring, talking on his phone—"he's making something else for me. Arrangements."

CHAPTER

37

I had told Sophie Gershowitz that I always got the dates right, on history tests, always got As. That was true. But I had never really got it, never understood history, how things fit together, because I needed someone to tell me the stories not of politics and dictators, but of berries and bunnies and books. Of how things are lost, and what that means and how it hurts.

In order to understand how it feels to say goodbye to your dearest friend, you need to know about a flowered apron, a Jell-O mousse, an old refrigerator with ice trays, and a whistling teakettle. You need a size-small T-shirt that says *Live Long and Prosper.* You need a yardstick.

Maybe you *above all* need a yardstick, because you have to measure everything so that it fits together, because you have to aim for an understandable ending.

My parents confirmed what I already knew. What I had feared, and dreaded, but knew. Aaron was moving his mother to an assisted living place in Akron. They said that they had looked at its website, and that I could do the same, and I would see that it was a lovely place, and she could have her cat with her, and there would be all sorts of things for her to do—a knitting group, movie nights, sing-alongs (sing-alongs! As if Sophie Gershowitz would ever *ever* go willingly to a sing-along!), even group trips to baseball games (and is there any team worth watching in Akron, I ask you?), and that she would be safe and content there.

At least they didn't say *happy.* Safe sounded good. Content? It's another form of happy, and probably as good as it would ever get for Sophie Gershowitz.

"Aaron's putting her house on the market," my dad explained. "He's staying over and an appraiser's coming in next week."

My mother chuckled a little. "Margaret Voorhees can start writing the brochure."

Actually, Oliver's mom got her start in the ad-writing business sooner than that. She created an ad that appeared in Tuesday's local paper:

> *No, it isn't a lie! This 1997 Oldsmobile*
> *Cutlass Supreme has only 10,000 miles*
> *on it! An elderly woman drove it only*
> *to the shopping center and back for*
> *all those years. It has a few tiny dents,*
> *because she wasn't great at parking!*
> *But everything else is in mint condition.*
> *Make us an offer!*

And someone did, on Wednesday morning. The new owner wasn't very happy, though. He was a boy about to go off to college, and his parents were giving him a car. He wanted a sports car. His parents said no to that—he was getting a good sturdy sedan, and if he ever got a speeding ticket they'd take it away from him so fast he wouldn't know what happened. He looked with a sneer at Sophie Gershowitz's car and said it was a codger-mobile and his friends would all laugh at him and if they wouldn't buy him a sports car, could he at least have a convertible, and they said no. They said take it or leave it. He made a face (you could tell that he was probably thinking, of his parents: *May lightning blast their crops and wolves fatten on their bones*) but then he grudgingly said okay and took it.

The appraiser came on Wednesday afternoon and wandered around with a clipboard, making notes. I watched through my own living room window.

Mr. Katz was lying on the back steps in the sun. While I watched, he lifted one paw, examined it, and then tended to it with his tongue. He ignored the appraiser, who carefully stepped around him and made a note when he noticed that the railing on the side of the back steps needed a repair. It was splintery and tilted a little. And the paint was peeling a bit on the house. With the car gone from the garage, you could see the cans of leftover paint where they sat on an abandoned workbench, but their lids were rusted; they'd been left there on the workbench too long. And probably a new owner would choose different colors anyway.

The outside of the house was painted a color called Roycroft Mist Gray, and the shutters were Bunglehouse Blue. We always laughed about that: *Bunglehouse Blue*! How could Sherwin-Williams have chosen such a foolish name? Sophie Gershowitz and I used to talk about starting our own paint company and how we would name the colors for things we loved. Gray would be, for example, Mr. Katz's Belly Gray. Blue would be Summer-Sky Blue. And there would be all kinds of reds: Rowan Berry for one. And—

While I watched, the appraiser took out a little penknife. He poked at the trim around the back door and some flakes of paint fell onto the doormat where I had wiped my feet a thousand times. He adjusted his glasses and made another note.

"Do you think the brochure will say fixer-upper?" I asked my parents.

"I bet anything Margaret Voorhees will come up

with some clever new phrase," my dad said.

"What does it mean, exactly: *fixer-upper*?"

"Just what it says," my mother said. "It needs work. New kitchen appliances, updated bathrooms, floors refinished, and—"

"That's superficial stuff," my dad pointed out. "To be honest, Soph, fixer-upper is what we say in the brochure. It sounds easy, and that's what we tell potential buyers: that they'll just need to paint the bedrooms, maybe put in a new kitchen floor, nothing very expensive. But the truth? Usually things need to be changed and redone from the very basics: new wiring, new plumbing . . ."

"New roof," my mom suggested.

Dad nodded, agreeing, and went on. "Structural work. Probably they should open up the walls and rebuild the foundation and give it a whole new structural integrity. Go back to the earliest construction flaws and make everything solid, and . . ."

I stopped listening. I didn't put my hands over my ears and hum *la-la-la* loudly. I didn't need to. My mind just went elsewhere. I began to fantasize that I could be a fixer-upper of the world. Not just slapping on new paint, but rebuilding the foundations of things, the way my dad said. I could go back to where terrible mistakes were made, and I would find the flaws, fix them, make things solid and right.

I would go to Poland and put the red berries back on the tree so that the time would be right and the jam would be sweet. I'd reconstruct the little house so that the people inside would be safe from the soldiers. In fact, I'd send the soldiers away! They would stay in their own country and I'd fix *them*, too, make them happy—if not happy, then content! The more I think about it, the more I think content might actually be better than happy—so that they'd never march into someone else's land.

I'd return the book of fairy tales. But this time the woman at the door would smile and invite the other woman in, and the little girls, and they'd read the fairy tales together in front of the fireplace.

And no one would ever get old. No, that isn't true—of course they'd get old, and become grandmas and grandpas. I'd fix it so that everyone had a grandma and a grandpa. But they'd be strong and healthy and their brains would work!

And I'd fix Oliver Voorhees. His brain would still be just as smart as it always was, and he'd know all the facts about practically everything, but he wouldn't need to twist his fingers together, and he'd be able to understand jokes, and he'd laugh at jokes and tells jokes to other kids so they'd be laughing *with* him and not *at* him, and he'd have friends for the first time, and there wouldn't be bullies anymore, and—

No, wait! Oliver Voorhees doesn't need fixing! He's perfect as he is. I would fix everybody *else*, everybody who doesn't take the time to understand Oliver, the ones who become impatient with him, the ones who think he's weird.

It is exhausting to think about it. There is so very very much to fix. And I know, of course, that a lot of it isn't fixable. I understand that.

But I can *try*. I'll start small.

CHAPTER

38

Turns out it is not as easy as I first described, to tell a story. One thing comes after another, and then the next thing happens, but then . . . something takes you by surprise. The story changes.

Sprinkling in a few adjectives doesn't help. You have to put in the feelings. That's the secret. That's the hard part.

You go to sleep beside your husband who has just retired from his job, and you think that soon you will travel and play bridge but then you wake up the next morning, and it is all over, all your plans are in pieces.

You walk down a snowy road beside your mother and sister and at the end of your walk you have turned into someone else, someone new and different, and everything has changed and you don't know why.

Blink, and things are taken away.

That happened in this story that I have just told to you.

But other things appear and surprise you.

That happened, too.

After he had gotten his mother settled in the passenger seat, and we had all hugged and said our goodbyes, Aaron Gershon handed me a package that he had set temporarily on the porch steps. "For you, my darling," Sophie Gershowitz said through the lowered car window.

I thanked her, and I was holding the package in my arms as he pulled out of the driveway. I shifted it to one side so that I could wave. Then the Accountant from Akron's car turned the corner so that I couldn't see it any longer and Sophie Gershowitz couldn't see me and so I stopped waving and I guess she probably stopped waving, too.

The future is still there, just different. You start figuring out what to make of it, and how to hang on to the memories of what has gone away.

Tree. Table. Book.

I went inside and opened the package. Then, after I had sat there for a few minutes (okay, full disclosure, I was crying a little), I called Ralphie.

"Mariani residence," he answered.

"*Ni-hao*," I said. (Chinese.)

"*Dobry den*," Ralphie replied. (Czech.) "What's up?"

"One. My mom says she can drop us off at the bowling alley this afternoon if you want to go bowling with me. She'll give us the money for shoe rental and everything, even some junk food if we want it."

"Yeah, and . . . ?"

"Two. Aaron is buying his mother a cell phone and he's going to teach her to use it, and my parents are going to get me one even though I'm only eleven, and Sophie Gershowitz will FaceTime me at ten a.m. every Saturday until I get married."

"Ha."

"Three. When I have a baby daughter, I am going

to wrap her in a soft white lacy shawl, which I am holding right here in my lap, and I will name her Shlomit and if anybody laughs at that I am going to punch them in the face and probably break their nose even though I am a nonviolent person."

"Got it."

He did, too. He knew right away which was a lie. That's because Ralphie knows that I hate bowling. The rented shoes are so weird-looking.

ACKNOWLEDGMENTS

I've written more than fifty books. Hard to keep count. One was written under an assumed name. Two were long-ago textbooks. Oh, and should I count the handwritten (and badly illustrated) one called "The Hippo in the Hollyhocks," which I made for my own young children a very long time ago? Anyway, more than fifty.

Most (all but "The Hippo") benefited enormously from editors and designers and all those publishing people who work so hard—and so competently—turning a writer's words into an actual book. I'm grateful, each time, for what they do.

But it occurs to me that there is a whole unnamed group of people whom I sometimes forget and rarely acknowledge: people whose books I have read, whose words have made me think, whose stories have influenced my own. *Tree. Table. Book.* owes a debt to Anita Lobel, whose autobiographical *No Pretty Pictures* begins with herself, a small Jewish child in a Poland newly occupied by the Nazis, being told not to look at the bloodstain on the sidewalk outside of her own home.

I'm grateful, too, to my friend Rachael Cerrotti, who wrote *We Share the Same Sky* to document her own grandmother's journey. Rachael knows both Poland and loss. She also knows about memory and how it becomes story.